"Aa!"

Winnie screamed so long and so loud that she felt as if her insides were being ripped apart.

"Win! Win!" she heard the director shouting. "You can stop now! That's a print!"

The director clapped Winnie on the back and grinned. "Thank you, Winnie. Your scream was awesome."

"Thanks," Winnie mumbled as she wandered away from the film crew. Her throat stung, and she was suddenly exhausted. Part of her wanted to keep on screaming forever, while part of her never wanted to make any sound again.

Back to my studies, Winnie thought as she collected her carpetbag and headed away from the plaza. *Back to the real world. Back to nothing.*

Don't miss these books in the exciting FRESHMAN DORM series

Freshman Dorm
Freshman Lies
Freshman Guys
Freshman Nights
Freshman Dreams
Freshman Games
Freshman Loves
Freshman Secrets
Freshman Schemes
Freshman Changes
Freshman Fling
Freshman Rivals
Freshman Flames
Freshman Choices

And, coming soon . . .

Freshman Heartbreak

FRESHMAN SECRETS

LINDA A. COONEY

HarperPaperbacks
A Division of HarperCollins*Publishers*

This is a work of fiction. The characters, incidents, and dialogues are products of the author's imagination and are not to be construed as real. Any resemblance to actual events or persons, living or dead, is entirely coincidental.

HarperPaperbacks   *A Division of* HarperCollins*Publishers*
10 East 53rd Street, New York, N.Y. 10022

Cover art by Tony Greco

First HarperPaperbacks printing: April 1991

Printed in the United States of America

HarperPaperbacks and colophon are trademarks of HarperCollins*Publishers*

10 9 8 7 6 5 4 3

One

....

"Winnie, come on," Faith Crowley urged. "Stop fooling around. This is my first day of working on a real movie. I'm nervous. I don't want to be late."

"You won't be late, Faith," Winnie bantered as she climbed the University of Springfield's Plotsky Fountain. "You're never late. You're never irresponsible or inconsiderate. You're never flakey or demented or weird or any of the other things that qualify as Winnie Gottlieb specialties."

"Oh, Win."

"It's okay, Faith." Winnie shrugged. "Know

thyself. Wasn't that in some play you studied this semester? Well, I know myself. After everything that's happened during the last few weeks, I know myself better than ever. I'm a motor mouth, a maniac, a flake, a fool . . ."

"You are not!"

"Trust me. I've lived in this body for a long time."

"Win, you're also funny and smart and original. Now let's go. I have to be at the movie location by eight."

"Okay." Winnie ran her fingers through her spiky, purple-dyed hair and jumped down from the fountain. She and Faith began to walk. They were heading all the way across campus to Mc-Claren Plaza. It was early, and dew covered the walkways.

"Lights! Camera! Action!" Winnie said dramatically. "That sounds so corny. Do they really say that?"

"Yes. I'm sure they do."

"Amazing." Winnie pretended to have been shot in the back, and she crumpled over a bike rack. The bells on her boots jangled. Her bracelets clacked. The Barbie dolls sewn to her book bag clunked.

"Come on." Faith quietly touched Winnie's back.

Winnie took a deep breath, laced her arm through Faith's, and touched her head to Faith's shoulder. "I'm coming, Mother Faith."

Faith shook her head. "Don't call me that, Win."

"Whatever. Lead on."

Together, they walked past the library and the Administration Building. The sky was clear and the mountains were visible in the distance.

Winnie pointed to Faith's Western Drama Festival T-shirt. "Maybe I should call you Director Faith. Hey, I guess you'd want everyone to know you're a theater-arts major this week. Maybe we should install lights on your forehead that say, 'Faith Crowley, U of S freshman and gofer on the first Hollywood movie to be filmed on our homey old campus.'"

Faith tossed back her braid and laughed. Her cheeks turned pink, and her fair skin glowed with excitement. "I still can't believe they're letting me work on this movie. The movie's producers asked for fifteen fine-arts students to help them during the week they're using the campus as a location. I can't believe I was the only freshman who got asked. I can't believe I'm going to get class credit for this. And I still can't believe they're really shooting a Hollywood movie at U of S!"

"I still can't believe that Santa Claus doesn't exist." Winnie began jogging backward, her Donald Duck earrings swaying in rhythm, her legs pumping steadily in bright red tights. They passed the student union, where people were lounging, flipping through textbooks, and sipping coffee. "So, do you know what the movie people are going to want you to do?"

Faith hugged her book bag. "I'm supposed to report to an assistant director first thing this morning for instructions. But my advisor said that I'm going to be working with a woman named Marion Becker. She's the casting director in charge of hiring all the extras for some big crowd scene. I guess I'll be helping her and anyone else who needs me."

"Sounds important."

"Yeah." Faith nudged Winnie, and the two girls hurried across the tree-lined driveway that led off to the Languages Building. "I'll be going for important sandwiches, sharpening important pencils, making important cups of coffee." She crossed in front of Winnie, taking a shortcut behind Powdermaker Hall. "It's a good thing we know each other so well. Otherwise, I might not even talk to you anymore—since I'm so important."

Winnie stopped cold. "Well, you wouldn't be the first high-school friend to decide you were too important for me."

Faith sighed. "Win. Don't."

Winnie took a deep breath and thought about how the third member of their high-school trio, KC Angeletti, had snubbed her and deserted her. KC hadn't even made the effort to come to Winnie's surprise birthday party the week before. Instead, KC had gone off with her snobby new sorority friends.

And if losing KC weren't enough, Winnie had also recently ruined things with Josh Gaffey, the boy she adored. After getting together with Josh and realizing that she loved him deeply, they'd broken up. The last time Winnie had run into Josh, he had been with a beautiful blond computer major named Sigrid.

Winnie hugged her stomach. Her love for Josh had turned into a giant black hole. No wonder she suddenly felt as if freshman year of college were a pointless joke. She had no major, no great interest in her classes, and no one to love. Trying to ignore the empty feeling inside, she followed Faith through a small patch of woods. Images of

Josh's gentle face, his single earring, his humorous smile, and the curve of his slender back kept coming at her.

When they finally got back on the bike path and went around the Continuing Education Center, Winnie began to jog, as if she could run thoughts of Josh and KC out of her head. "So, why did you want me to come with you this morning, other than to keep my mind off my disaster of a life?"

Faith jogged, too. "Winnie, I started to tell you why in the dining commons over breakfast."

"You did?" Winnie wrinkled up her nose. "I guess my mind was on something else. Besides, seven in the morning is not exactly the time of day when I'm most coherent. Tell me again."

Faith sighed. "Okay. The film people scouted a lot of universities for a location to shoot a big crowd scene that comes at the end of the movie. They picked U of S because they liked McClaren Plaza. Anyway, they'll be hiring a couple hundred students to be extras in the shot. They're interviewing students this morning and I thought you might want to give it a try."

"You know me. I'll give anything a try," Winnie replied. "Would I have to act?"

"I don't think so."

"Well, who are all the student extras supposed to be?"

"Students." Faith laughed. "The movie's a comedy about a graduate student who's invented a way to contact UFOs. He installs some weird device on the roof of the Physics Building and has a romance with a girl from outer space."

"Perfect. *Hey, aliens!*" Winnie yelped to the sky. "*Take me with you!* Maybe my life will work better on Mars." She ran a hyper little circle around Faith. "What's this movie called?"

"*U and Me,*" Faith answered. "That's with a "U" , not a Y.O.U."

"Could have fooled me." Winnie took off in a sprint, leaving Faith behind. When she passed the medical school and turned onto McClaren Plaza, she stopped in her tracks.

"Oh my God!" Winnie gasped, staring at the square. "This is major stuff."

McClaren Plaza was a brick-paved square dotted with cherry trees and surrounded by the oldest buildings on campus. Usually it was a quiet place to sunbathe or read, but that morning it looked like a cross between a street fair, a Winnebago lot, and a truck stop. Pickups, semis, and RVs lined three sides of the square. Men and women carrying clipboards and walkie-talkies dashed back and forth. There were piles of lights, poles, and electrical cable. A sign at the entrance of the square said, "Interviewing for extras today. Please form a line here." Beyond that, a line of what looked like at least three hundred students snaked around the square.

Faith finally caught up while Winnie stood and gawked.

Winnie whistled. "Hey, it looks like the Martians have already landed. There are so many people here! Maybe I should skip this and go back to my dorm."

"What for?" Faith objected. "So you can crawl into bed and feel sorry for yourself?" She grabbed Winnie's hand and pulled her into the plaza. "Come on."

Winnie went.

Faith dragged her past the students in line, pausing to wave to some friends from the theater-arts department. "I wonder how so many people found out about this?" she questioned, almost to herself.

Winnie mumbled a chorus of "I Heard It through the Grapevine." Soon she started to do a dance and clap her hands. She continued to dance until she and Faith had almost reached the front of the line. Then she put a hand to her mouth and clammed up. She grabbed Faith's arm. "You didn't tell me that KC was going to be here, too!"

"I didn't?"

"Faith . . ."

"I guess I didn't think of it," Faith stammered.

"Yeah, sure," Winnie scoffed. She stared at her ex-friend. KC was almost at the front of the line. She was wearing her usual dress-for-success finery, her briefcase resting on the ground and a library book in front of her face. Just looking at KC's long dark hair and beautiful, perfect face made Winnie feel like her insides were shutting down. "KC is such an overachiever, she's even at the front of the line."

Faith cleared her throat. "So maybe you should go stand with her. Then you won't have to wait so long."

Winnie turned to face Faith. "So that's what this is about? You went through this whole thing just to get me and KC back together?"

"No. I want you to be in the movie. I want you both—"

Winnie glared at Faith, who broke off in mid-sentence. Then Winnie turned back to look at KC again and felt even worse. "It won't work, Faith. Look who's with her."

"Who?" Faith spoke in a whisper, craning her neck to see into the growing crowd.

"Courtney Conner. Miss Tri Beta Sorority. KC's new best friend."

At the same time, KC turned and noticed them.

"Hi, KC. Hi, Courtney," Faith shouted as she took Winnie's arm and eased her all the way up to where KC and Courtney were standing.

"Hello," Courtney said, smiling graciously. The president of the Beta Beta Beta was blond and elegant. She was wearing an impeccably tailored skirt, silk blouse, and a short black jacket.

KC barely looked up from her book.

"It's okay if Winnie cuts in line with you, isn't it?" Before anyone could reply, Faith added, "Of course it's okay. I have to go. I'm supposed to report to some assistant director person." She grinned and backed into the crowd. "Good luck. Bye!"

"Goodbye," Courtney said with a smile.

"Thank you so much, Faith," Winnie whispered sarcastically.

After Faith was gone, a long silence followed. Everyone else in line around them was chatting and laughing, but Winnie felt as if the world had just gone perfectly still. KC kept her nose in her book, as though looking Winnie in the face would contaminate her, especially in front of Courtney.

"So . . ." Winnie said. She rocked on her heels and the bells on her boots jingled. "Here we are."

Although Winnie had seen Courtney from a distance, they had never actually met. Winnie stuck out her hand to shake. Her nails were bitten and red. "Winnie Gottlieb."

Courtney extended her perfectly manicured hand. "Courtney Conner. Very nice to meet you." Courtney stared at Winnie's hair.

Winnie patted her head, making the spikes stand up even more. "Great hair, huh?"

"It's purple," Courtney said softly.

Winnie made herself smile. "I dyed it last week, in a fit of self-destructive mania, as my mother the shrink would say. Hey, maybe you should try it! But I think pink would be more your color."

Courtney gave an uncomfortable laugh.

KC still wouldn't lift her eyes from her book. It was driving Winnie crazy, so she did what she always did when she was about to go out of her skin: she talked. "Hey, speaking of my mother the shrink, KC knows my mother. KC and I went to high school together. Did you know that, Courtney?"

Courtney shook her head.

"My mother the shrink—actually, she's not technically a shrink, she's a family therapist—anyway, my mom is coming to visit Springfield soon. Did I tell you this, KC?"

Now KC's book completely covered her face.

"I guess I didn't." Winnie continued to chatter while Courtney stared at her. "But she is coming. My mom, I mean. She's giving a speech to some place downtown called the Crisis Hotline." Winnie laughed. "I don't know why I'm telling you this, Courtney, except that I thought you might want to know in case you were a psych major or you thought you were about to have a nervous breakdown or something."

Courtney's brown eyes widened.

"Just a joke," Winnie blurted. "Of course you're not going to have a breakdown. People like you only have breakthroughs, or whatever you call them. Now people like me, we have breakups, breakdowns—"

"Winnie," KC suddenly warned.

Winnie stepped back in shock and put her hand to her forehead. "She speaks!" she gasped. "I thought maybe that book was glued to your nose, KC. If it were any closer, you'd have been reading it cross-eyed. What book could possibly be that fascinating?"

KC finally dropped the book. "It's *Wuthering Heights,* if you have to know. I'm doing an extra-credit paper for my English composition class on the psychology of Heathcliff. I'm trying to finish reading it."

KC's book started to go back up, but Winnie was unable to control her mouth. She turned back to Courtney. "*Wuthering Heights!* Great book! It's about this wild guy, Heathcliff, who falls madly in love with Cathy. I wrote a paper on it in high school. I called it 'Heathcliff, One Messed-Up Dude.' I got an A."

KC huffed. Then she glared at Winnie, her gray eyes cold and unforgiving.

Winnie looked away. For the first time she noticed that the line had begun to shuffle forward. About ten feet in front of them, beyond the first five or six students, was a table laden with papers, clipboards, and boxes of file cards. A hiply dressed black woman wearing sunglasses and a baseball cap had sat down and was arranging everything neatly in front of her. Another student helper, who Winnie recognized as Faith's friend Merideth, bent over to talk to the woman. Then

Merideth picked up a stack of cards and began passing them out to everyone in line.

"Everyone take a card," Merideth projected. "Fill in your name, address, and phone number, and have it ready when you get to the front of the line. Here we go!"

There was a burst of applause and then nervous quiet as the first two students sat down in chairs across from the woman, chatted with her for a moment or two, then got up and walked away. The line chugged forward again.

"Hey," Winnie couldn't resist adding, "Faith told me that they call this kind of audition a cattle call." She grinned at KC and Courtney. *"Moooooooo. Moooooooo."*

KC flinched. Courtney gave an overly polite smile. Winnie tried not to scream. They stood like that, without another word, until the line moved and moved again and it was Winnie's turn to sit down at the table.

"Next."

"Me?" Winnie asked. "Just me alone?"

The woman behind the table glanced at KC and Courtney, then nodded at Winnie. She wore a name tag that identified her as Marion Becker, the casting director. "Just you. Have a seat, please."

Winnie sat down, leaving KC and Courtney behind her. She handed over her address card.

Ms. Becker looked at Winnie's card. "I'd just like to ask you a few questions, Winnie. We need to find students who we can clearly identify as different types for this crowd scene. I want to find out a little bit about you. What are your interests?"

Winnie shifted in her seat. "History. Guys. Running. Guys. Traveling. Guys." She shrugged. "That's kind of a hard question."

The casting director laughed. "What's your major?"

"That's an even harder question." Winnie glanced back at KC and Courtney. They were chatting to each other, ignoring her completely. "I'm undeclared. While I'm searching for a major I can live with, I'm looking for something I can't live without . . . or someone."

Marion Becker wrote something down on Winnie's card. "I see. Can you afford to miss classes this Friday morning?"

Winnie stared at her. "You mean I'm in the movie? That's it? That's all there is to it?"

Ms. Becker nodded. "That's all there is to it. Now don't get too carried away. You're only going to be an extra, and it'll be hard work. But you will be paid twenty-five dollars and it should also be fun. Someone will call you later in the week with further instructions."

Winnie grinned and clapped her hands. She started to stand up. "Is that all for now?"

"Almost," Ms. Becker said. "The only other thing we need is a Polaroid picture of you for our files." She pointed to a short line that had formed in front of a trailer about twenty feet away. "Step right over there and get your picture taken, and then you can go on your way. We'll see you again on Friday."

"Okay. Wow. Great. Hey, maybe college isn't so bad after all. Thank you."

"Thank you, Winnie."

Winnie started to get up and head for the picture line, but then she glanced back at KC again and hesitated. "Ms. Becker," she said in a softer voice, "do you mind if I ask you one thing?"

Ms. Becker shook her head. "What is it?"

Winnie bit her lip. "You said before that the extras were supposed to be different types. Um, I don't mean to pry or anything, but what type am I?"

Marion Becker gave her a big, warm grin. "Oh, darling, you are a wacko. A perfect wacko!"

"That figures," Winnie muttered.

Two
....

KC watched Winnie leave Ms. Becker's table and disappear. Immediately after that, Ms. Becker got up to take a phone call, so everyone on line was enjoying a little break. KC didn't care if they broke until noon. She put her copy of *Wuthering Heights* back in her brief case and sighed. She needed time to get herself together.

Courtney took the opportunity to check her face in a small gold compact. She delicately powdered her nose. "Your friend Winnie is certainly different."

"Different?"

Courtney smiled. "Interesting."

Sure, thought KC. *Just like traffic accidents and earthquakes are interesting.* Now that Courtney had met Winnie, KC wondered if the fact that Winnie and she knew each other would hurt her chances of becoming a Tri Beta. She figured that she was already on thin ice after making a fool of herself a week earlier when Marielle Danner had gotten her drunk just before a Tri Beta tea. She wondered if Courtney still wanted to be seen on the same campus with someone whose friends looked like Winnie. "Winnie and I are old friends." KC shifted. "Very old friends. You know how that is."

"What exactly do you mean?" Courtney asked in a surprisingly direct voice.

"Oh, you know how things change," KC hedged. "People change. High-school friendships fade. Especially when you get to college."

"I've always valued my old friends."

"Yeah. Me, too," KC backtracked. "It's just hard sometimes."

"I like Winnie, KC," Courtney insisted. "She's original. She's funny. And she's a little sad."

KC wasn't sure what to say. She liked Winnie, too. Actually, she loved Winnie. Winnie had always been there to cheer her up, just like the time KC had gotten fired from her very first sales job at the Jacksonville Mall. But all that had been a long time ago—before college, before the Tri Betas, before KC had decided that if she wanted to get ahead in life, then some people were going to get left behind.

"Winnie's okay." KC took a deep breath. "She's had a rough time lately. She broke up with her boyfriend. I guess it's been pretty hard on her."

Courtney nodded.

Luckily, Ms. Becker returned to her desk and KC was glad not to have to go into any more detail about why Winnie was so unhappy. She and Courtney both stood up straight and waited to be called.

Ms. Becker quickly sorted through her papers, then looked up at KC, who was the next in line. Ms. Becker stuck out her hand and KC handed her the address card.

"Sorry to make you wait," said Ms. Becker. "I had to take a call from Alec Brady's agent."

KC glanced back at Courtney and smiled. Alec Brady, the star of *U and Me,* was one of the hottest young actors around.

"We understand," Courtney assured Ms. Becker.

"Of course," KC added hastily.

The casting director stared at KC, then at Courtney, then back at KC. "Why don't you two girls sit down together?" she suddenly suggested. "I'm trying to type my extras and I think we have two of the same type in you girls."

KC and Courtney sat next to each other in the gray metal chairs. Courtney handed over her card, and they waited for Ms. Becker to ask the first question.

Ms. Becker called over her shoulder, "Peter darling, if you're finished with all the kids waiting over there, just join me and take Polaroids of the students while I interview them here. I think things will go faster that way."

"Okay, Marion," answered a wry male voice. "Whatever you say. You're the boss."

KC's heart stopped. That voice! She looked around and saw the face and body that went with it. It was Peter Dvorsky, a talented sophomore photography major who was obviously helping on the film, too. He had shaggy light brown hair and green eyes. Dressed in an old sweatshirt, jeans, and a vest that flapped open, Peter looked as unimpressed by the movie as he always was by KC. He stood behind Ms. Becker, then recognized KC and stared at her with his amused, challenging eyes.

"Well, hello," Peter said with a grin. "Look who we have here."

KC cleared her throat.

"You know each other?" Ms. Becker asked.

"You could say that," Peter tossed back in his usual flip style.

KC stared at him. She had dumped Peter as her Winter Formal date because she had thought he was too ordinary, going instead with a guy who was gorgeous, but who had turned out to be shallow and dull. KC regretted that decision, but her regret wasn't something she wanted to admit to Peter.

"Hello, Peter," she said, cool as ice cream. "Nice to see you."

"And you." Peter studied her. His eyes seemed to look right into her soul. "Hey, Courtney, how are you?"

"Fine." Courtney smiled.

"How do you all know one another?" Ms. Becker asked.

Peter raised his camera and shot a quick Polaroid of Courtney. "I've taken their pictures before. I was the photographer for a university calendar. KC and Courtney posed for it. Actually

KC was the business consultant for the whole thing."

"I'm a business major," KC said.

Peter nodded. "It was a surprising success."

"Why surprising?" KC couldn't resist challenging. "Because I worked on it?"

Peter grinned as Courtney's photo came out of the camera. He looked at it, then stapled the photo onto Courtney's address card. "I never said that, KC. It was just surprising. Every experience I've had with you has been full of surprises."

Marion Becker seemed to be enjoying their exchange. She leaned forward on her arms. "Actually, I'm glad that you two girls have had some experience in front of a camera, even if it's a different kind of camera. I can already tell that I'd like to use both of you in the movie. I have to admit that you two are practically perfect examples of a certain type I'm looking for. You're almost too good to be true."

KC felt her tension melt a little. She liked being compared favorably to Courtney.

Ms. Becker made a few notes on her clipboard. "Are you both available later this week?"

Courtney reached into her leather bag and pulled out a neat, slim appointment book. She consulted it carefully. "It depends. On Thursday

I have a meeting with my sorority alumnae. I can't miss that, I'm afraid. That night I have my international relations study group. And Saturday is the Providence Ball." Courtney looked at the casting director. "It's where we raise money for the children's hospital. My parents gave me two tickets and I guess I'd better go."

Guess she'd better go! KC had read about the Providence Ball in the paper. It was the biggest, richest, showiest social event in all Springfield. Society people came from all over to raise money for the renowned Providence Children's Hospital, which was affiliated to the university's medical school. The tickets cost at least a thousand dollars each, and Courtney's parents had sent her two! KC's parents, who scraped by running a tiny health-food restaurant in Jacksonville, could barely afford to send her a pair of tickets to a Grateful Dead concert. KC would have given her entire semester's meal ticket to get an invitation to that ball.

Ms. Becker checked a stack of papers. "So far, it looks like the crowd scene will be shot on Friday. So we won't interfere with your busy social schedule. You won't need to miss anything except your Friday morning classes."

"That sounds fine." Courtney leaned back in

her chair and crossed her long legs. "I'm doing well in all my classes, so it won't matter if I miss a few."

KC wished she could say the same. She was struggling to pull C's. Her paper on *Wuthering Heights* was for desperately needed extra credit. She had to get her average up before spring rush or she'd never make the Tri Betas' grade requirement.

Ms. Becker gave KC a nod. "You can miss a few classes as well, I assume?"

"Of course," KC lied. "No problem." Peter kept studying her as Marion Becker jotted some notes on a card. KC refused to look back at him. She was sure that he could read every crazy thought that was scurrying across her brain. *I'm barely passing my classes. I hope Courtney likes me. I wonder how deeply I hurt Winnie this time. And what is Peter thinking when he stares at me like that?* KC tried hard to make her face as calm and gracious as Courtney's.

"Well, that's great," Ms. Becker told them. "One of my student assistants will call you in a day or two to give you all the information about the shoot. I think all we need is a photo of . . ." She squinted as she read KC's full name on the card. "Is it Kahia Cayanne?"

KC wanted to crawl under the table.

"What a charming name," Ms. Becker said.

"Yeah. I guess you could say that." KC loathed the full name her hippie parents had given her. She'd only written it out on the card because they said they wanted legal names, along with Social Security numbers, so that they could issue paychecks. KC wondered what Courtney thought of her real name, but Courtney seemed preoccupied, checking her watch as if she were late for an important appointment.

Ms. Becker gestured for KC and Courtney to stand up. "Peter, why don't you take Kahia aside for her photograph, while I go on to the next interview? Thank you, Courtney. Thank you, Kahia. I'll see you both on Friday."

"Thank you, Ms. Becker." KC slowly stood up while Courtney said a quick goodbye and rushed off. Then she moved out of the way of the next interviewee and found herself face to face with Peter, a few yards away from Ms. Becker's table.

Peter held up his camera and stepped closer. Film-crew people and potential extras were bustling back and forth, but somehow all the hubbub made KC feel like she and Peter were alone.

"Say cheese, Kahia," Peter teased.

"Just call me KC, thank you," KC barked back.

"I haven't called you at all," Peter came back.

"I never expected you to call me, Peter. Believe it or not, I don't sit around by my hall phone, thinking about you."

"I never said you did."

KC made a face.

Just as she narrowed her eyes and scrunched up her mouth, Peter snapped her picture. "Lovely," he teased, then checked back to make sure that Ms. Becker was occupied while he waited for KC's photo to develop. The casting director seemed mesmerized by a swim team jock who had the words *U of S* shaved on the side of his head.

Peter finally pulled KC's picture out, examined it, and snickered. "Guess we'd better try again." He handed the photo to her. "It's a good thing you have pull with the photographer, or you'd have to go down in movie history looking like this."

KC cringed. In the photo, her mouth looked mean and pinched. Her eyes looked defensive and impatient. "Well, if you didn't try and make me angry, I might not come out looking so awful."

"KC, don't blame me for how you look," Peter

said. "I'm just the photographer. I'm just the mirror showing the world what's really behind the makeup and the pretty clothes."

"I'm not blaming you." KC forced a smile and Peter took another shot. "I just wonder why you have to be like this all the time. Why can't you ever say, 'KC, how nice to run into you! Gee, you look nice. You seem to be doing well'?"

Peter laughed and looked at the photo. "Gee, KC," he said to the photo. "You look great. You seem to be sort of okay. And I really am glad to run into you."

KC softened a little. She glanced at her second photo, which was somewhat better. "Thanks. Same to you." For a moment their eyes locked, and KC got a scary feeling that Peter could take her in a different direction from all her ambitions and plans.

"Peter!" Ms. Becker suddenly interrupted. "Are you through with Kahia? I'm sending you another extra. He goes in the jock file."

Peter took a few steps back toward Ms. Becker. "I'm ready, Marion. By the way, what type were KC and Courtney? Which file should I put them in?"

"They're the bored beauties," Ms. Becker said,

without looking back. "Perfect casting, don't you think?"

Peter looked back at KC. "I don't know," he said. "I hope not, but I've never been quite sure."

Three

....

By that afternoon the line of potential extras was gone, but Faith was still there, sitting at Marion Becker's table in the middle of McClaren Plaza.

"Did you finish filing those names by type, Faith?" asked Ms. Becker, pointing to stacks of three-by-five cards.

Faith looked up. "I'm done, Ms. Becker."

"One hundred and seventy-five eager college students ready to sacrifice their GPAs for one brief, shining moment of cinematic glory."

Including one wacko and one bored beauty, Faith

thought. *Maybe Winnie and KC are too different ever to be friends again.*

Ms. Becker smiled and leaned against the table. "Are you having a good time working with us?"

Faith grinned. "Fabulous."

"You're doing a wonderful job, Faith."

"Really, Ms. Becker?"

"Call me Marion. So far, all you U of S students have been just great."

"Thanks."

"Thank *you*, darling." Marion Becker finally took off her sunglasses and rubbed her eyes. "I'm going to go make some calls. Why don't you wander around and see if anybody else needs some help?"

"Okay, I will."

Faith waited for Ms. Becker to leave, then stood up and stretched. She looked around the square, deciding where she would wander to first. At first she had just stood around gawking at everything, but now she was beginning to feel comfortable with the layout. Equipment trucks containing cameras, lights, dollies, poles, and miles and miles of electrical cable lined the north side of the plaza. The other technical trailers—makeup, sound, wardrobe, and props—sat along the east side. And on the west edge were the trailers that belonged to the actors.

"Alec Brady and Elizabeth Seymour," Faith said to herself as she dodged a sound technician and began to walk in the direction of the wardrobe trailer. She had glimpsed the two stars earlier in the day, while they were rehearsing for a shot. They had both looked shorter than she'd expected, paler, and more . . . well, normal. But still, small-town Faith Crowley had actually laid eyes on Alec Brady and Elizabeth Seymour! Faith could list all of their films and even the guest shots they'd done on her favorite TV shows.

Faith stuck her hands in the pockets of her overalls and walked past the catering truck, from which wafted smells of sugar doughnuts and coffee. Suddenly, she heard a deep voice holler from a location area that had been set up near the corner of the square. There were poles and lights all around, and the actual area for the shot was surrounded by heavy drapes.

A script girl suddenly took off her glasses and shouted, "Can I get one of those college helpers to run an errand for me?"

Faith raced over, her cowboy boots clattering against the ground. "Can I help you?" she asked, showing the identification badge that was pinned to her overall bib. When she tipped the badge so that the script girl could see it, the pin broke. Faith quickly plucked her badge off and stuck it in her pocket.

The script girl nodded. "Check with wardrobe on the color of Alec Brady's shirt in the exterior shot with the college president. Wardrobe changed it yesterday."

"Right away." Faith spun around, facing the line of trailers that stretched along the east side. She took off, stepping over the mounds of tape and wiring.

When she reached the edge of the plaza, she checked the closest trailer. Peering in, she saw the bright lights and barber chairs. "Makeup," she reminded herself. The makeup girl pulled herself away from the mirror and waved.

The next one should be it, Faith thought. And as soon as she got to the door, a voice confirmed her suspicion.

"Too tight! If I wear this suit, my body mike will become a permanent part of my anatomy."

Faith poked her head around the corner and saw the heavy-set character actor who was playing the college president. He was being fitted for a pinstriped suit.

"Sorry, sweetie," said the wardrobe mistress. She was on her knees and had safety pins and straight pins stuck all over her shirt. A measuring tape was draped around her neck. "Let me check the inseam."

Faith stuck her head in. "Excuse me. What color was Alec Brady's shirt in the exterior shot with the president?"

"Green," the mistress shot back. "That's forest, not kelly or moss or olive or jade."

Faith nodded. "Got it." She popped back out of the trailer and ran back to the technician, weaving among light poles and ladders. Then she relayed the message and wandered back to Marion's table.

By the end of the day, Faith had run at least a half-dozen more tasks: finding the correct pronunciation of a Spanish word, relaying personal messages from Marion's husband, delivering specially flavored antacid, getting the weather prediction for that night, and determining the availability of seven Yorkshire terriers for the next day's shoot. Faith was neatening Marion Becker's casting lists, when an older woman with stylish gray hair and glasses approached her. Faith remembered Marion telling her that the woman was Alec Brady's personal secretary.

"Are you one of our U of S helpers?" the woman asked.

"That's me," Faith assured her.

"Can you do one more thing before you go home?"

"Absolutely." Faith had no interest in going home. Her day had been so exciting and fun that she could have stayed in the plaza forever. The last thing she wanted was to go back to Coleridge Hall, do homework, and worry about KC and Winnie.

The woman smiled. "Mr. Brady wants two bottles of Calispell mineral water delivered to his trailer. Trailer number one, of course." She reached into a leather coin purse. "Here's some money. I don't know where you can get the water at this hour."

"I do. They sell it at the store inside the student union." Faith's breath stopped for a moment. It had just hit her that the conclusion of this errand would be a visit to Alec Brady's trailer.

"Are you all right?" the woman prodded.

"What?" Faith rocked on her cowboy boots. "Oh, I'm fine."

"Good. Thanks so much."

"Thank you!" Faith cried as she took off again

on her way to the student union. The thought of meeting Alec Brady made her feel as if she were jet-fueled, as if she could run forever.

Racing back past the library, Faith thought about how glad she had been to get away from Winnie and KC that morning, how relieved she had been to escape the tension and irritation that surged back and forth between her two friends. Being around them lately was like getting stuck on a barbed-wire fence.

As Faith ran into the student union she thought about how she wanted to celebrate. After all, she had just finished her first day on a movie set. Her life was full of wonderful, rewarding work. She wished Winnie and KC's lives were as happy as hers right now.

"Two bottles of Calispell, please." Faith told the girl at the student-union snack store. Part of her still wanted to do everything possible to bring peace between Winnie and KC, but another part of her wanted to start worrying about herself for once! Hadn't she put in a lot of work planning a surprise party for Winnie, only to have KC not show up and Winnie leave feeling more miserable than ever? It just didn't seem worthwhile to spend all her energy on efforts that went unappreciated.

"Thanks," Faith said to the girl, taking her change and her bag of water bottles. She brushed back some stray hairs that had escaped from her French braid, tucking them in at the back of her neck. Hugging the bag, she started to run back.

She smiled as the plaza came into view. Now she was going to meet Alec Brady.

"Ahhhhh," she squeaked.

A few yards before Alec's trailer, she took a deep breath. *Alec Brady,* she told herself. *Just a man, a human being on the planet Earth, a guy with two eyes, a nose, and a mouth.* Then she bantered back and forth inside her head. *Sure. Right. Just handsome, talented, rich, funny, famous, brilliant, successful Alec Brady. About the most extraordinary human in the entire world.*

Faith took a few steps. By the time she reached the door to the star's trailer, her hands were damp and her heart was going like a jackhammer. She lifted her hand to knock, then paused.

That was when she heard two voices arguing inside.

"Let's discuss this, Alec!"

"Let's not discuss it, Fred. As far as I'm concerned, the issue is closed."

Faith hesitated. Then she knocked, but no one

seemed to hear. Not sure what else to do, she put her hand on the door. It swung open.

"Alec, baby, listen to me."

"Fred, *baby*, I've listened to every word you've said. I just don't like what I've heard."

Faith froze in the doorway. Alec was arguing with the film's director, Fred Gorman. Neither man seemed to notice her, so she was able to stare shamelessly and really take Alec in. His reddish hair was short, straight, and a little messy. He looked younger than she would have thought, and more tired. His face was refined, actually more handsome than on screen, with deep-set eyes and a sensitive, full mouth. Faith remembered a slight dimple appearing when he smiled, but, of course, he wasn't smiling now. He was furious. In chinos and a sweatshirt that said *U and Me,* his fit, muscular body looked like it was aching for a fight.

"The shot was scheduled for today," Fred argued.

"The shot was scheduled for first thing this morning," Alec yelled back. "And you told me we were postponing it until tomorrow. Now you suddenly change your mind and tell me I have to do my hardest scene at six o'clock with no preparation and no rehearsal. It won't work, Fred. Forget it!"

"Come on, Alec, baby," Fred wooed. "The light is perfect. Be reasonable!" He tried to put his arm around Alec's shoulder.

Alec Brady shook the hand off as if it were a tarantula. "I'm not a baby, Fred. I don't have be reasonable about this and I don't care about your stupid light. You can't ask me to turn on my most emotional scene at the end of the day, when I'm not prepared, just to save your producers a few bucks. I won't do it!"

Fred huffed.

"That's it, Fred," Alec grumbled. "That's my answer. Now get out of here and leave me alone."

Fred shook his head, then stepped past Alec, heading toward the trailer door. "All right, we'll shoot it first thing tomorrow," he conceded.

"Thank you," Alec spat out.

Pushing Faith out of the way, Fred barreled past her and went out.

Faith stood there for a few seconds listening to her own shallow breathing. Meanwhile, Alec kicked his sofa, then fell onto it. He muttered to himself.

Faith tried to take a step forward, but her legs wouldn't move.

"Jerk," Alec said out loud. "It would just cost him more in retakes. Or else he'd use the shot and make me look like a fool. He'd eat me alive if I let him. They all would."

Faith stepped forward. She wondered if her voice would come out. "Um, excuse me."

Alec looked up. When he saw her, his face turned red with fury. "Who are you?"

Faith's heartbeat went into double time. A hot flush crept up into her face. "Hello."

"Did Fred send you?"

"Fred?"

"I told him no and I meant no. How hard is he going to push me this time?"

"Fred didn't send me. I don't even know him."

"Than how'd you get in here?"

"I walked in. Your door was open."

"Oh, great," Alec said, falling back on the couch with his head in his hands. "Just what I need. Look, if you want an autograph, I don't give autographs."

"I—"

"And if you want to stare at somebody, go to the zoo."

"I'm sorry."

"I'm sorry, too. But I've had a long day and I'd like some privacy. Please go away."

"I've had a long day, too," Faith heard herself say.

He barely acknowledged her. "Yeah, I'm sure you have."

Faith just stood there, hugging her paper bag and staring even harder.

"So what are you waiting for?" he demanded. "Are you going to refuse to leave my trailer? Maybe you're planning to find my hotel so you can crawl into my bed and wait for me?"

"What?"

"And you'll probably show up on location tomorrow and yell and wave while I'm trying to concentrate."

Faith finally remembered that she wasn't wearing her identification badge. No wonder Alec thought she was some kind of star-struck groupie! She awkwardly tried to fish her identification badge out of her pocket. "You don't understand. I'm—"

"You're nobody," Alec grumbled.

His words stung her. Faith was surprised to feel a surge of hot anger. Finally she found her badge, but the pin had caught in the lining of her pocket and she was unable to pull it out. "I'm Faith Crowley."

"So nice to meet you, Faith Crowley," he replied sarcastically. He walked toward her. "Now, Faith, go back to where you came from." He grabbed her arms and guided her back to the doorway. "You can tell all your friends how you met Alec Brady and what a terrible, mean guy he was. Or else you can make up a story about what a great guy I am and what a wonderful time we had together. I don't care what you say, as long as you leave me alone."

Something inside Faith snapped. She had decided not to take inconsiderate behavior from KC and she didn't know why she was taking it from Alec, movie star or no movie star. She struggled out of his grasp, then shoved the bag of mineral water into his arms. "For your information," she railed, "I'm part of the crew. I'm one of the U of S assistants. I know I'm not important like you, but I've been working all day, too. I'm not even getting paid!"

Alec's blue eyes opened wide with astonishment.

"That's your mineral water," Faith continued. "Two bottles of Calispell. Your secretary asked me to get it for you." She reached in her pocket. "And here's your change."

"I didn't—"

"You're welcome, Mr. Brady," Faith blurted before he could say anything else. "I've always wanted to meet you. But now that I have, I can assure you that it was a real disappointment."

"Wait—"

"*You're* the nobody, Alec Brady," Faith said to herself as she stumbled down the steps and ran back out into the perfect spring evening. It wasn't until she was halfway across McClaren Plaza that she began to cry.

Four

························

SCCRREEEECH. *Rattle. Rattle.*
SCCRREEEECH. Rattle. Rattle.

The printer spat out paper as Josh Gaffey stared at the computer screen. All around him, the Bradley Computer Center buzzed with activity. Bright lights shone down on busy students tapping away at keyboards, talking with partners about projects, making decisions about projects, and debugging programs. In front of him, the cursor on the computer screen beat time. It pulsed like a heartbeat, rhythmic, regular, steady. There were no flutters, no jumps, no excited pounding—not like his own heart these last few weeks.

Obviously the computer had never met Winnie.

"Josh? Josh?"

Sigrid Anderson, Josh's lab partner from Computer Science 212, laid a hand on his shoulder, then let it travel down his back. He looked up into Sigrid's face. Her skin was rosy and her long blond hair shone. Even her polo shirt, khaki shorts, and loafers looked well taken care of.

"Yes, Sigrid?" Josh smiled weakly.

"You okay?" She kept her hand on his back and played with the long wisps of hair that curled down his neck. "Our project for the Computers in Business class is due next week, and we're only half finished. It's Tuesday already. What are you thinking about?"

Bad question, Josh thought. He was thinking about Winnie again, picturing her big, sad eyes, her kooky smile, her wild hair, and her small, taut body. "I'm not thinking about anyone," he sighed.

"Excuse me?"

"I mean, anything. I'm not thinking about anything."

"Well, we both need to think about this assignment." Sigrid slid into the chair beside him, snuggling up and giving him one of her seductive, lean-on-me smiles. Gazing at the screen, she nodded. "You seem a little distracted, so let's work together. We still need to set up columns showing the different fields, different corporations, and the range of benefits and salaries."

"Okay." Josh took a deep breath and went back to the keyboard. "Here we go."

The project was to create a program that would compare different corporate careers by salary, benefits, security, and possibilities for advancement. Josh didn't find the subject very interesting, but Sigrid had chosen it with such enthusiasm that he'd had no choice but to go along with it. Just as he'd gone along when she'd chosen him as her lab partner.

He squinted a little, trying to remember what he'd just typed. Then he stared at the screen.

Sigrid reached across him, her shoulder pressing against him as she pushed the scroll key so she could review what he'd just done. "Hmm."

"Let's print it out," he suggested.

"Good idea."

Josh touched a few keys and the printer began to clatter loudly, giving him a headache. Sigrid looked over the graphics as soon as the paper emerged from the printer.

She smiled and murmured, "Very nice." She showed him the pages. "Josh, you've got such talent."

Yeah, he thought. *Talent for not knowing why I'm doing what I'm doing. Talent for losing the girl I can't seem to forget.* Then he grimaced and told himself not to think about Winnie. That was the whole point of spending time with someone as together and strong as Sigrid. He was going to make a radical change in his life and find a new direction.

Meanwhile, Sigrid bent over the desk, making corrections on the printout. Josh made himself notice that she had a great figure. Sigrid was tall and athletic with wide shoulders and shapely legs. And yet the more Josh stared at her, the more she made him think of a high-school gym instructor or a professional bowler.

He smirked.

"What's funny?" Sigrid asked, noticing his sudden smile.

Josh didn't know quite how to tell her that she'd made him flash on *Bowling for Dollars*. Winnie would have had no trouble with an observation like that, but somehow he didn't think that Sigrid would take it the right way. "Never mind."

Sigrid smiled, too, and leaned toward him. "You know, you would make a great marketing analyst. With your computer background, all you would have to do is add marketing skills and practically every corporation would be drooling over you. You should consider changing majors."

"I'm computer science all the way, Sigrid. I can't help it. I'm just a nerd at heart. I'm one of those guys who'll end up building robots in his basement."

Sigrid laughed and playfully slapped his arm. "You are not. And besides, freelance computer designers are so flakey. There's no security. You might as well be a musician."

Ugh, thought Josh. The word *musician* made him think of Travis Bennett, the guy Winnie had met in Europe, and who had briefly come to Springfield, trying to rekindle his summer romance with Win. Travis had been a musician, and his reappearance in Winnie's life had caused the breakup between her and Josh.

Sigrid perched on the desktop, crossing her bare legs. "It's never too early to think about your future, Josh. I went to this seminar where they talked about picking a corporation or two and then tailoring your coursework to their needs and specialties. See, different corporations are looking for different areas of expertise. That's why you should have these things figured out as early as you can."

Josh hastily printed another copy of their work, and the printer's rattle and screech drowned out Sigrid's voice. What Sigrid said made sense, he told himself. Still, that sort of planned-out existence made Josh want to jump out of his skin. He might like to program computers, but he didn't want to become one himself.

"Josh," Sigrid said insistently.

Josh didn't respond.

"Josh." She was standing over him now, reaching for the keyboard.

"What?"

Sigrid leaned over, punched a few keys, then showed him the latest pages to come out of the printer. For some reason, the second copy he had printed was gibberish. He must have given the computer some crazy command and had gotten a haywire response.

"I'm sorry, Sigrid," Josh stammered. "I don't know what I did."

Sigrid leaned her head against his and sighed.

"It's too stuffy in here, that's all. You're not in the mood to work. I understand. We'll finish this another time. Let's go out and get some fresh air."

"Okay." Josh gave in, pushing away from the desk. He rubbed his face. That was the problem with being chaotic and thinking about *Bowling for Dollars!* Assignments never got done. And thinking about Winnie certainly didn't help.

Sigrid began massaging Josh's shoulders. Then she picked his leather jacket up off the chair and helped him into it. "Let's go out and take a long walk. We can even look at the some of the houses right around the university. I hear the real-estate values are really going up, and maybe we can get an idea of what's out there. Then we can stop at this new seafood restaurant just past the Beanery. What do you say?"

Josh looked into Sigrid's determined blue eyes and didn't say anything. He didn't know what to say or think or do anymore. So he let Sigrid take his arm and start to lead him away.

He pulled back only when he noticed that the computer they had been using was still on. He reached over and flicked the switch off. He watched the screen go black. *Okay,* he thought.

That's it. Delete Winnie file. Work out a new program with Sigrid.

"She's ready, Courtney."

"But am I?"

"Are you?"

"I guess so. I'd better be ready." Courtney folded her hands. "Send her up."

"I will."

"Thank you, Diane."

Diane Woo, the vice president of the Tri Beta sorority, stepped out of Courtney Conner's bedroom, which was on the second floor of the lovely Tri Beta sorority house, and quietly shut the door.

As soon as Diane was gone, Courtney spoke to herself. "I'm not looking forward to this. This is not going to be easy."

Courtney sat at her desk while her clock ticked and the breeze rustled her curtains. Nervously she leaned to look out her window at the BMWs and Volvos parked along Greek Row. The big sorority and fraternity houses were equally impressive with their columns and porches. Impressive, too, were the attractive and well-dressed students who lived on the row and who sat chatting and laughing on the houses' front stoops.

Courtney loved being president of the best sorority on the row. She loved the Greek system of sisterhood, in which selected girls lived together in a big, grand house. She loved her tiny bedroom and the Tri Beta common areas, which were always filled with decorations and flowers.

And yet at that very moment Courtney would rather have been anywhere else besides Sorority Row. She would rather have been at the ordinary student union with her nonsorority friend, KC. She would rather have been in McClaren Plaza watching the movie crew, or downtown shopping for the Providence Ball. She would even rather have been in a K Mart than waiting to say goodbye to the sorority sister who had just been kicked out of the Tri Beta house—the soon-to-be ex–Tri Beta, Marielle Danner.

"Marielle," Courtney whispered, "I'm sorry this had to happen so cruelly, but I can't say I'm sorry to see you go."

A few moments later, footsteps stomped up the carpeted hallway, followed by a violent knock on Courtney's door. Courtney cringed at the sound of Marielle's charm bracelets rattling as she continued to pound. Before Courtney could open the door, Marielle let herself in with such force that the bulletin board on the back of Courtney's door almost flew across the room.

Without a word, Marielle threw her weight onto one hip and crossed her arms in front of her. She was dressed in pleated trousers and a scoopnecked lambswool sweater. Her lipstick and nail polish were bright red, accenting her brown hair and fair skin. Courtney gestured for Marielle to sit down on her bed. "Please, have a seat, Marielle."

Marielle plopped down with a defiant toss of her head.

"How are you, Marielle?"

Marielle simply glared.

Courtney sat up straighter. "I felt it would be best to say our goodbyes in the privacy of my room. I didn't want any kind of a scene in front of the other sisters."

"Whatever you say, Your Highness," Marielle came back in her twangy voice.

Courtney sighed. "Marielle, do you understand why we had to take this drastic step?"

Marielle shrugged.

"You accepted our rules when you pledged this house," Courtney recited. "We prize our values, and you betrayed them. You tried to sabotage KC Angeletti's chances of becoming a Tri Beta by going over to KC's dorm room before she was due at our Tri Beta tea, and getting her drunk! You know that we want KC to join this house after spring rush, and yet you deliberately set out to humiliate and hurt her!"

Marielle checked her nails. "Spare me the speeches, Courtney. Just tell me to get lost and let's get this over with."

Courtney felt her anger rise. Very few people could make her lose her temper, but Marielle had always gotten to her. For two years she had been forced to accept Marielle as a member of her sorority, even though Marielle stood for everything Courtney disliked. Marielle was conniving and snobbish, petty and mean. Of course, she was also rich, pretty, and well connected, which was why she'd gotten into the Tri Betas in the first place. Courtney loathed Marielle, but her upbringing wouldn't allow her to show anything but politeness. "I gather that you are moving out this week."

"You gather correctly." Marielle played with her charm bracelet and looked sullenly around the room.

"Have you found another place to live?"

Marielle laughed. "You'll be happy to know

that the only place I can find midsemester is in the drecky dorms."

"The dorms aren't so terrible," Courtney said.

Marielle stood up. "Yeah? Well, I don't see you voluntarily dropping out of the Tri Betas and moving back on campus. Look, Courtney, let's cut the games. I don't like KC. She's from some weird, flaky family and I think it shows. She's not good enough to be a Tri Beta. I don't like you either, for that matter, so maybe it's a good thing that I am going.

Marielle's voice had trailed off, and Courtney suddenly realized that Marielle was on the verge of tears. "Marielle?"

Marielle put a hand to her face, then pulled herself together and continued. "Not that I want to leave this house," she went on. "But I obviously have no choice." The tears sprang down Marielle's cheeks and she pointed at Courtney. "But if you think I'm going to just take this and disappear, you're wrong! You may have kicked me out of the Tri Betas, but you haven't seen the last of me, Courtney. I promise you!"

Courtney had almost started to cry, too.

"Oh, please. Don't give me your phony sympathy!" Marielle shouted. "You pretend you care about the girls in this house, but you don't. And

I've got news: they don't care about you, either!"
Marielle pushed the door open and ran down the
stairs.

Courtney could hear Marielle's frantic footsteps thumping through the sorority living
room. The last thing she heard was the front
door being slammed shut. For a moment Courtney leaned toward the window again and
watched Marielle fleeing down Sorority Row.

"Good riddance," Courtney said, trembling.
She stood up, clutching her dresser as she
checked her image in the mirror, making sure
that her eye makeup was intact, before going
downstairs.

But just before Courtney got to her door, she
felt something cave in inside. Something deep
inside had come up with unstoppable force. She
wasn't sure why, but she began to sob, then
dropped onto her bed and pressed her face into
her pillow so that none of the other girls would
hear her.

"Why am I crying?" Courtney gasped.

She thought back to the movie-extra interviews, to the tension between KC and Winnie,
and to Winnie's eccentric behavior. Despite the
obvious anger between the girls, Courtney had
been able to feel a deep bond. She had felt it

when Faith was with them, too. She envied that sort of connection. She even envied Winnie's nuttiness.

"Just once," Courtney wished out loud, "I'd like to be friends with someone just because I like them, not because of who they know or how much money their parents have or even what sorority they belong to."

Courtney thought about KC. She admired KC's beauty and her desire to get ahead. She liked KC's business smarts and sensed that KC's shell of toughness covered a soft, generous inside.

Without realizing she had done it, Courtney had already opened her address book. She flipped through it, wondering how many of the phone numbers belonged to real friends, and how many were just society acquaintances and contacts. Then she flipped to the A section, picked up her phone, and dialed.

A girl answered. "Langston House, can I help you?"

"KC Angeletti, please."

"Just a moment."

Courtney settled back onto her bed, hugging her pillow and cradling the phone.

"Hi, Faith," KC said in a friendly voice. "I've

been waiting for you to call and tell me how it's all going on the movie. Hey, have you talked to Winnie since the casting interviews?"

"KC?"

"Oops. Who is this?"

"It's Courtney."

"Oh. Courtney. How nice of you to call."

Courtney slunk down further on the bed. She hated the way that KC's casual tone had vanished, replaced by a tone that was much more nervous and unsure.

"Have you heard anything from the film people?" KC asked.

"Not yet."

"Neither have I."

There was a silence, and Courtney wondered why she had called. Then she remembered: to take a chance, to make a friend. Suddenly an idea popped into her head and for once she didn't weigh the options or formulate the proper way to say something. "KC, you know those two tickets my parents gave me for the charity ball?" she blurted.

It took KC a moment to respond. "Yes."

"I'm not dating anyone right now and I assumed I'd take Diane or one of the other girls from the house."

"Of course."

"But just now it occurred to me that *you* might like to go."

"Me?"

"Not that charity functions are all that interesting, but it's for a good cause and we get to dress up and have a nice dinner. So . . . well, KC, do you think you'd like to go?" Courtney was surprised to find herself as edgy as if she were asking a guy out on a date.

"Are you serious?" KC finally responded in a low, stunned voice.

"Of course I'm serious, KC. It's this Saturday night."

"Oh, Courtney! That's unbelievable!" KC cried. "That's fantastic. I'd love to go!"

Five

·········

Winnie lay back on her dorm room floor the next morning, crinkling candy wrappers, potato chip bags, notebook paper, and old magazines beneath her as she did fifty sit-ups.

There was no doubt about it. Her side of the room was disappearing under a mountain of junk. As Winnie stood up, she kicked a muddy running shoe out of her way, reached across the mound of books, and drove her arms into the pile of clothes on the bed. She pulled out her wrist weights and strapped them on.

"Maybe I should clean this place up," she muttered as she started arm circles. "Maybe I could start a business project and be a successful young entrepreneur, like KC."

Winnie pushed harder, rotating her arms and groaning from the pain. "Front, two, three, four. Back, two, three, four."

Get past KC, she told herself, trying to shake off the terrible anxiety that was eating at her. *Life goes on and things change. Get over the fact that KC is embarrassed by you. Get over the fact that Josh has another girl.* Winnie circled and pumped until her shoulders throbbed. Then she crumpled down on the floor and rested.

That was when the memories started nagging at her again and voices started popping in her mind. She imagined Faith lecturing her. *Get interested in your classwork, Win. There are other things in college besides Josh.* Then her mother's voice chimed in. *I can't wait to see you when I visit Springfield to talk at the hotline, hon. I know you're just doing so well now.* Josh's humorous voice added, *It's probably a good thing that Travis came between us. We would never have stayed together anyway.* And then there was KC, who didn't even have a voice lately, just an intolerant glare behind a library copy of *Wuthering Heights.*

"I should have hung out with Heathcliff,"

Winnie muttered. "He'd probably be the only guy messed-up enough to put up with me."

Winnie finally got up, ripped off her tank top and wrist weights, pulled on a wrinkled hot pink sweatshirt, and grabbed her Western Civ book. She had another half-hour before class. Maybe she could actually study. She could only hope that the Italian Renaissance would succeed where obsessive exercise failed. Maybe Machiavelli, the Medici family, and Galileo would silence the annoying voices.

Winnie yanked open her dorm-room door, checking the long hallway for signs of Josh. He, too, lived in Forest Hall, only ten feet away—too close for comfort when she wanted to avoid him, and too far away when the only thing she wanted was to throw herself into his arms.

"Good," Winnie whispered.

Stereos were blasting, the showers were on, and a guy down at the end of the corridor sang the school song in an off-key voice. There was no sign of Josh or his roommate, Mikoto. "All clear. Maybe Josh is out with that big blond, getting compatible and exchanging floppy disks."

Winnie raced down the hall, then hurried down the stairs, skipping three at a time until she made it to the basement. Then she sped past the laundry room and the candy machines, heading for the study cubicles. Since Forest Hall was such a party dorm, the basement study room was usually empty. Winnie herself hadn't studied much over the last few days. She was hoping to sit in a cubicle for twenty minutes and at least stare at her textbook.

Finally she reached the study room and opened the door. But when she saw who was already inside, she gasped. Every muscle in her body went rigid.

"Win."

"Oh. Hi."

"Uh, this is Sigrid."

"I know."

"Hi there! Did Josh say your name was Lynn?"

"Win. Short for Winifred."

"How nice."

"What's nice about it?" Winnie asked Sigrid. "That you thought my name was Lynn or that my real name is Winifred?"

"Both." Sigrid gave her a blank smile. "Either one."

Josh and Sigrid were lumped together over a stack of computer paper, with Sigrid's long hair actually draped across Josh's slender back. Winnie stared at Josh's woven bracelet, his single blue earring, and his T-shirt with bleach spots. The sight of him made her ache from the ends of her dyed hair all the way down to her toes. She held back tears and thought the effort of keeping herself together would make her insides explode.

Sigrid still looked confused. "Anyway, it's very nice to meet you."

Wish I could say the same, Winnie thought.

Josh stared back at Winnie. For a moment she thought she saw a sadness in his eyes, an emptiness that almost matched her own. Then she shook her head and backed into the doorway.

"I'll guess I'll just go on to my class," Winnie mumbled. "I didn't really want to study anyway."

Josh stood up. "You can use the room. We're almost done, Win."

"No we're not, Josh," Sigrid said, lifting her arm and lacing it around Josh's waist.

Winnie stared at Sigrid's arm as if it were a poisonous snake.

Sigrid smiled. "Josh, we still have to figure out how to cross-reference the corporate health and pension plans, plus the investment benefits."

Josh's face had a pained expression.

"You go right ahead," Winnie said. "That sounds very important. Health-plan and pension yourselves away. That's very real-life. Much more real-life than Florence and the creepy Medicis. Don't mind me." She kicked the door open and stepped back out.

"Win . . ."

"I'm gone," Winnie sang. "Just think of me as a commercial break in the docudrama of real life."

Clutching her Western Civ textbook, Winnie turned and ran across the basement, up the stairs, and out the dorm's back door. Continuing her breakneck pace, she sprinted across the dorm green, dodging volleyball games and floating Frisbees. Then she raced past the Computer Center and Mill Pond, behind the University Theater, and around the library until she found herself sitting in an empty corridor, waiting for the class before hers to let out so that she could go into the lecture hall for Western Civ.

"What's happening to me?" Winnie mumbled. "Why am I such a maniac?" She hugged herself and watched the wall clock. "And why do I say such dumb things all the time?"

A few minutes later, classroom doors opened one by one and students began to pour into the hall. Winnie waited a while before trudging into Western Civ and finding her seat, which was always near KC, Faith, and Faith's roommate, Lauren Turnbell-Smythe.

Faith wasn't there. KC and Lauren were already sitting together talking, so Winnie wiggled into the seat on Lauren's right. Lauren was dressed in a loose sweater and parachute pants, holding some notes on what was probably an upcoming article for the *U of S Weekly Journal,* the college newspaper. As soon as Winnie sat down and looked at KC, the conversation between KC and Lauren ended.

"Where's Faith?" Winnie asked Lauren, trying not to look at KC, who was hiding behind *Wuthering Heights* again.

"She's still working on the movie," Lauren answered in her soft voice.

"Oh. Right," Winnie said. "Everyone seems to disappear when you really need them."

KC briefly glanced over.

"Faith is missing classes all week," Lauren added. "KC said that you and she and Courtney are going to be extras on Friday. Is that right?"

Winnie shrugged.

"I think it sounds great." Lauren nudged her. "You know, Faith met Alec Brady."

"Really?"

Lauren shrugged. "She said he was kind of a jerk."

"Gee, I guess there's no monopoly on being a jerk these days," Winnie grumbled.

KC closed her book. "What is that supposed to mean?"

"Nothing."

KC frowned, then leaned forward in her seat, as if she could talk to Lauren alone and pretend that Winnie was invisible. "Anyway, Lauren," she confided, "like I was saying before, I think I can get by with my dress from Winter Formal, but I'm not sure exactly how dressy this charity ball is. Do you think I could borrow—"

"Why don't you just ask her if you can borrow her life, KC?" Winnie interrupted, referring to Lauren's wealthy parents and fancy-boarding-school background. Even though Lauren hated the pressure of coming from a highbrow family, Winnie knew that KC envied it all.

"Winnie, do you mind?" KC hissed.

"Sorry."

Lauren gave Winnie a sympathetic smile, then glanced back at KC. "You can borrow my pearls, KC, and my shoes, too, if you want." Lauren paused. "You know, it's pretty unusual for someone like Courtney Conner to ask a non–sorority member to an event like that charity ball. I'm really surprised."

KC leaned back with a smug smile. "I know. I couldn't believe it when she called."

Winnie sank lower into her chair. *Great. So now KC and Courtney are so close, they're saving hospitals together.* Winnie was beginning to feel so raw and alone that she started into one of her motor-mouth monologues, even though she saw Dr. Hermann pulling down his maps and getting ready to start his lecture.

"Lauren, did we ever tell you about the time in high school when Faith, KC, and I all got sick at the same time?" Winnie chattered.

Lauren shook her head.

"Not that we ended up in a children's hospital or anything. Well, actually, only Faith and KC got sick—they had some exotic flu from Hong Kong—but I pretended to be sick and stayed home, then sneaked out to the store. My mom is divorced and works as a shrink all day, so I could kind of do as I pleased—actually that's still true, I kind of do whatever I please and my mom just thinks I'm experimenting and I'll learn from my own mistakes, which she says is okay with her."

KC took out her notebook with an tight expression on her face.

Lauren continued to smile.

Winnie rambled on. "So I waited until Faith's mom had gone out and KC's parents were at their health-food restaurant, and then I picked up KC and drove her and all this weird food over to Faith's, where we made chocolate-marshmallow burritos in the fireplace. They were supposed to be s'mores, but I forgot to buy graham crackers and Faith's mom had tortillas in the kitchen. We had a really great time."

"Winnie," KC said. "Can't you ever shut up?"

Winnie looked down and saw Dr. Hermann surveying the lecture hall with a scowl.

"So after that, whenever any of the three of us was sick . . ." Winnie continued in a softer voice.

"Winnie, be quiet," said KC.

Dr. Hermann cleared his throat.

"We'd get together after school . . ."

"Win, shh," Lauren finally urged.

Dr. Hermann looked right at Winnie and tapped his hand on the lectern. "Could I have quiet, please?"

Winnie leaned toward Lauren. "And we'd have a chocolate-burrito attack!"

At the same time Lauren and KC repeated, *"Shhhh!"*

Dr. Hermann frowned and launched into his lecture.

"Okay, okay, okay," Winnie said, feeling as if she'd been slapped. She slid down in her seat.

Pens scribbled obediently, and notebook pages rustled. Winnie sat and stared. Inside, she was boiling over. KC and Lauren took notes furiously, as did every other student in their row. But Winnie couldn't write. She couldn't listen. She couldn't think. Dr. Hermann's voice faded and his face blurred before her.

"Perhaps the greatest of Florentine painters was Leonardo da Vinci," Dr. Hermann droned on.

Winnie waited a few more minutes. She tried to concentrate, but it was useless. Dr. Hermann's voice faded again. Winnie glanced over at Lauren, who was poised over her notes. She leaned forward and looked at KC, who was staring down at the professor, her face as perfect and immovable as a marble statue.

Suddenly Winnie scooped up her books and stood up. Her seat snapped up behind her and there were whispers all around.

"Sit down."

"Hey!"

"I can't see."

Winnie stumbled past twenty pairs of knees, ignoring KC's angry glare. She dropped her textbook and stepped on a girl's foot. Finally she tripped into the aisle and ran out into the hall. Flying out of the building, she wanted to be as far from KC and that lecture hall as possible. Maybe there was a hole she could fall into, a marathon she could run, a freighter to China she could hop on and never be heard from again.

Crossing the grassy common in front of the student union, Winnie headed into the brisk wind. She leaped over flowerbeds filled with primroses and tulips until she found herself in McClaren Plaza, near one of the walls of movie trailers and the strange swarm of cast and crew. Then she collapsed onto the bricks and opened her Western Civ text. An empty blue book fell out.

"Maybe I should write about how I feel," Winnie told herself. She found a pencil and began spilling her confusion onto the page. All her feelings about KC and about Josh, about Faith and Lauren and Melissa and Brooks, and all the other people whose lives seemed so on track, poured out across the blue lines.

And then she started writing about the only person she could think of who was as big a screwup as she was: Heathcliff, that messed-up dude from *Wuthering Heights*. For some reason, it made Winnie feel a little better to sit on the bricks for an hour and write about him.

Six

"Hello. Is this Penny Cameron?"

"It sure is. Who's this?"

"This is Faith Crowley. I'm calling to remind you about the movie shoot on Friday."

"Did you think I'd forget? It's only written in twelve-foot-high letters on my calendar. Six A.M., McClaren Plaza."

"Good. Now you're a hippie type, so Wardrobe would like you to wear a tie-dyed T-shirt and blue jeans."

"No problem. That's what I wear most every day."

"Great. Thank you. See you then."

That evening, Faith was using the phone in the political-science office, which had been set up to serve double duty as a production office for the movie crew. For three hours straight, she'd been phoning the students who were going to be extras in the shoot. Her neck hurt, her ear felt twisted, and she was starting to lose her voice.

And yet she was content. Actually, she was more than content as she looked over her list and checked off Penny's name. She was delighted to be out of the plaza, in a place where there was no chance of running into Alec Brady again. And she was overjoyed to still have her job. She was amazed that after what had happened with Alec Brady, she hadn't been dismissed from the movie crew and told never to come back.

Faith dialed another number. "Hello?" she said as someone picked up.

"Rapids Hall," announced a cheerful voice.

"Can I speak to Richard Carlyle?"

"One second. *Richaaaaarrrrd!* Get your bod to the phone, dude!"

A moment later another voice said, "Yo."

"Hi, Richard. This is Faith Crowley. I'm a student assistant on *U and Me* and I'm calling to remind you about the shoot on Friday. McClaren Plaza, six A.M."

"No way I'd forget. They told me to ask you what I'm supposed to wear."

Faith checked Richard's card. "You're a jock type, so that means they'll be supplying you with a costume when you get here. A football uniform, I think. You might bring a raincoat, though. The forecast says there's a fifty percent chance of rain."

"No problem. Hey! I'm going to be a star."

"I'm sure you will. See you on Friday."

Faith rubbed her eyes. That had been her last call. The fluorescent lights above her hummed, and she got up, stretching out the crick in her neck. She still had that I-don't-want-to-leave-here feeling, so she looked for things to do. She attacked the coffee makers, emptying the pots and scrubbing the brown film off the insides, and refilling the baskets with dry coffee. Then she crossed to the windows and pulled one open.

Moving back to her desk, Faith piled the casting cards neatly on one corner and made a note to call the car dealerships first thing in the morning about getting an old Volkswagen for Elizabeth Seymour to drive. As a poor student, Elizabeth's character walked most places, but there was one scene where she needed to borrow a friend's car, and the production designer said she had to borrow an old, dinged-up Volkswagen.

Faith ran her hand over the stacks of scripts and pages of rewrites, as the silence around her deepened. When she finally realized that there was nothing else left to do, she went back to the closet for her fringed suede jacket. But then she stopped, as she heard a door squeak somewhere down the hall. The sound echoed through the empty building and then footsteps approached, tapping along the linoleum floor. Faith felt her heart pound uncomfortably in her chest. She put her head up, listening. The footsteps stopped right outside the office and the door opened.

Faith turned. She was shielded by the closet door and couldn't help hiding as Alec Brady sauntered in.

"Oh no," she mouthed. Her heart had dropped down to her stomach.

"Hello?" Alec called as he entered. He wore a long-sleeved burgundy polo shirt tucked into old, faded Levis, high-tops, and an expensive-looking watch. His hair was messy again. He glanced left and right, then smiled when he found the pile of scripts on the production desk.

The famous dimple appeared in his cheek as he sorted through them.

"Anybody in here?" he called out as he continued to flip through the scripts. "Hey, Stockman, I'm supposed to get the new pages for tomorrow. Are you around? Are these them?"

Faith swallowed. She considered hiding all night, but then Alec sat down, as if he was going to wait, too.

"Stockman," he called again.

Faith accidentally made a noise as her jacket buttons brushed against the metal closet door. Alec looked over.

She gave him a weak smile. "I'm the only one here right now, Mr. Brady."

Alec looked right at her but his face didn't change. Faith wondered if he remembered her. Maybe with all the adoring fans who'd thronged the location and forced the crew to put up barricades, with directors, producers, and wardrobe and makeup people to keep straight, with lines and blocking to remember, he'd forgotten her completely. After all, he did think she was a nobody.

Alec watched her as she slowly walked back over to her desk. He stood up but seemed reluctant to leave. He pushed some papers around the unit manager's desk, then leafed through a shooting script.

Not knowing what else to do, Faith put her jacket on, as Alec whistled. She headed for the door.

"Well, uh, I guess I should just leave Stockman a note," Alec finally said in a funny, uncomfortable voice.

Faith froze.

"Maybe he can send the new pages over to my hotel," he continued.

Faith nodded and went back over to her desk. "I'll make sure Mr. Stockman gets your message." She gestured to a pad of message slips on top of the production desk.

Alec scribbled on one, then handed it to her.

Faith couldn't stand the suspense any longer. Was Alec pretending not to remember her? Was he just waiting for the most dramatic moment to let her have it? Had their encounter been so unimportant that he had completely wiped it out of his memory?

She flipped back her braid and looked him in the eye. "Look, Mr. Brady . . ."

At the same time, he began, "Look, I . . ."

"I'm sorry," Faith blurted. "Excuse me. You were about to say something?"

"No, excuse me," he insisted. "What were you going to say?"

Faith cleared her throat. "No, you tell me. I mean, please finish whatever you were starting to say."

An embarrassed flush crept over Alec's cheeks. "No. You go ahead, please."

Faith shifted. There was an awkward pause. "Okay. I'm really sorry about coming into your trailer uninvited yesterday. It wasn't really my fault, but I can understand how you might have misunderstood."

Alec picked up a pencil and tapped it on the desk. "I did misunderstand. Which is probably why I should be the one to apologize."

"Well . . ."

"I wasn't exactly in a great mood when you came in."

"I still shouldn't have come barging in like that. At least I could have knocked."

"Well, I shouldn't have automatically assumed that you were some crazed fan," Alec assured her. "You must think I'm the world's biggest egomaniac."

"You must think I'm pretty nervy."

Finally he took a moment. He shrugged and smiled. His dimples formed two deep creases in his cheeks. "Well, you may be right on that one. You were pretty nervy."

For some reason Alec's smile relaxed Faith and made her feel nervier still. "Well, maybe I think you're an egomaniac."

His smiled widened. "I am."

"What?"

He sat on the corner of her desk. "It's pretty hard to become a successful actor and not be an egomaniac. I'd just like to think that I'm not a total jerk, too."

For the first time Faith was beginning to suspect that he really wasn't a jerk at all. "I guess I *am* kind of nervy." She smiled.

"I'll say." He stuffed his hands in his pockets and his eyes took her in.

Faith blushed. "I'm sure that kind of stuff really happens, though. I mean, people bugging you and wanting your autograph. Except for— well, did some girl really sneak into your bed at your hotel?"

Alec made a face and nodded. "While I was shooting *Reversing Roles*. She refused to leave. I had to call the police."

"You're kidding."

"I'm not."

"How did she get in?"

"She bribed the hotel manager. She told him she'd get him one of my sweaters for his daughter if he'd let her into my room."

"Oh no!" They both laughed.

After that they were quiet and Faith started to feel shy again. "By the way, my name is Faith."

"I know. I remember."

"You do?"

"Faith Crowley, right?"

"Really? I mean, yes, you're right. That's my name."

He stuck out his hand to shake. "I'm Alec."

"I know." She took his hand. As soon as the handshake was over, she felt embarrassed and started to pull her hand back. He held on a moment longer.

"Nice to meet you, Faith," he said, looking into her eyes.

"Nice to meet you, Alec."

They stared at each other until Alec finally let go. Faith felt as if she were suspended in midair.

Alec suddenly laughed, sounding like he was feeling a little giddy, too. "So, Faith, do you mind if I hide in here with you for a few minutes?"

"Of course not." Faith glanced out the window at the hubbub still going on in the Plaza.

The sunlight was slipping away and they were setting up for some night shots in front of the Law Center. "Hide as long as you like. Are you avoiding more crazed fans?"

He sighed. "Actually, I'm avoiding my director. And I'm avoiding some public-relations person that came up from the studio today. I'm also avoiding my agent, who's been trying to reach me, and a half-dozen reporters who've been hanging around my trailer. Sometimes there are so many people on a movie set who want something from me, I don't know how they think I'll have anything left to give to the film." He rubbed his face, then looked at her. "Sorry. I'm being a jerk again. And a bore. I'm just talking about myself. I'm sure this doesn't interest you at all."

"Yes, it does," Faith reflected. For some reason what he'd said had made her think about KC and Winnie. "I even know what you're talking about, at least I think I do. Of course, I've never had reporters and agents after me, but sometimes I feel like my friends expect so much of me that I don't have anything left for myself. Could that be the same thing?"

"Could be." He leaned back with a serious expression. "Tell me more about it."

"About what?"

"About your friends."

She connected with his eyes again and felt a wave of self-consciousness. "You don't really want to hear about them."

"Sure I do." He laughed. "Believe me, hearing about your friends has got to be a lot more interesting than hearing about how my dimples looked in yesterday's rushes, or what Elizabeth Seymour's next job is going to be, or how my hair is always such a mess."

Faith hesitated. When he continued to smile at her, she took a deep breath. "Okay. Well, I have these two best friends who I went to high school with named Winnie and KC. We were this terrific, inseparable trio when we were younger and we even made it through our first semester of college okay. But now KC and Winnie are drifting apart. And I guess I feel like the one in the middle, the one who has to keep us all together, no matter what."

He nodded, listening intently.

Faith went on. "Except that lately I've started to feel like I can't always stay in the middle and try to hang on to both of them. Because if I do, I'm going to get torn in half."

When she finished speaking, she noticed that

Alec was staring down at his hands with a sad expression. Then he got up and walked slowly over to the open window.

"I don't know why I told you all that," Faith backtracked, suddenly feeling foolish. "I'm sure it has absolutely nothing to do with what you were saying."

Alec stood with his back to her for a few minutes. A cool breeze came and ruffled the papers on the desk.

"What are you thinking?" she dared to ask after the long silence.

Alec kept his back to her. "I'm thinking," he answered, "that if you're going to let people tear you apart, it makes a lot more sense to have those people be old friends whom you love, rather than people who are just using you so they can make money." When he finally turned around, Faith saw a vulnerability in his eyes that she had never seen before, not even on screen. But a moment later Alec had covered that vulnerability with his magazine-photo smile. He clapped his hands and moved away from the window. "Anyway, it's getting late. I'd better go before I really start to bore you."

"You're not boring me," Faith responded.

He tapped her arm. "I have a four A.M. makeup

call tomorrow, so I'd better go anyway. I have to be asleep by eight-thirty. Isn't an actor's life glamorous?"

Faith laughed.

Alec made his way to the door, then stopped and turned back around.

"Don't worry," Faith assured him. "I won't forget to give Mr. Stockman your message."

"I know you won't." Alec looked down and kicked aside a piece of crumpled paper with his sneaker. "You know, Saturday's the last day of shooting on this movie. There's a wrap party that evening to celebrate the end of the film. I think the producers are planning to invite all the college students who worked on the film."

Faith nodded. Her friend Merideth, another college helper, had already told her about the party.

"I usually don't like wrap parties very much," Alec rambled. "Everybody stands around congratulating everyone else and worrying about their next job. But I thought I might go to this one. I wondered if you might want to go with me."

"With you?" she mimicked blankly. It was as if he'd just spoken to her in Swahili.

"Yes, with me. Unless you already have other plans."

"No, I don't have any plans."

"Great." He smiled. "So I'll see you on Saturday night. I may have to meet you at the party if it rains and my last few shots get changed around. But we'll still go. Okay?"

Faith grinned.

"Great." Alec ducked back into the hallway and waved. "See you Saturday."

"See you then."

Faith waited until she was sure that Alec had left the building. Then she jumped up and down, tossed her neat stack of cards into the air, and let out an ecstatic scream.

Seven

··

"**I** shouldn't be here," Faith insisted as she lounged around the dock of Mill Pond the next afternoon. She was sunbathing with KC, Lauren, and Lauren's boyfriend, *Weekly Journal* assistant editor Dash Ramirez. All around them swimsuit-clad students splashed, played tapes, and lay on towels catching some rays on this warm spring day.

"I've missed so many classes this week," Faith went on. The minute I had some free time, I should have gone right to the library."

"I don't want to hear that you should be studying instead of gossiping with us," bantered KC, who sat up very straight, her face tilted to the sun. "Not when you actually have a date this weekend with Alec Brady."

"That's right," agreed Lauren, who sat back, leaning against Dash. "If you don't tell us everything about Alec, none of us will ever speak to you again."

"I'll still speak to you," Dash offered with a sly smile.

"I've already told you everything there is to tell," Faith said, beaming. "The movie's producer gave us the whole day off today, so I can't get any more dirt for you until tomorrow."

"Why did you get the day off?" asked Dash.

Faith undid her braid and ran her fingers through her hair. "It's suppose to rain tomorrow and over the weekend," she explained, "so the movie people are shooting as many exterior scenes as possible before then. Today they're filming in front of some bookstore downtown, and they told all the college helpers to take the whole day off. Is that perfectly clear?"

KC shook her head and pounded the wooden dock. "We don't want clarity, Faith. We want gossip!"

"That's right," Lauren agreed. "We want juicy gossip."

KC and Lauren laughed and started talking at once.

"Are Alec Brady's dimples for real?"

"I heard he's even shorter than he looks on screen."

"Does he like business majors?"

"Did he really go out with Candice Hurley?"

"Does he really own a red Maserati?"

"Come on, Faith. Inquiring minds want to know!"

Dash looked around at the girls, then propped himself up on one elbow. He had a bandanna tied around his forehead, and his wavy dark hair stuck out from under it. "You females are shocking."

Lauren bopped him on the head with her notebook.

Dash rubbed the bruise. "Hey, maybe Lauren and I should write an article about Brady. The headline could read: 'Handsome Young Movie Star is Actually Five Thousand Years Old.'"

Lauren punched him playfully in the stomach.

Dash held up his hands. "'Movie UFO Turns Out to be Real Thing. Alec Brady Has Two-Headed Baby with Innocent U of S Freshman.'"

"Dash!" Lauren giggled.

"Would you guys stop?" Faith pleaded, hiding

her face in her hands. "I hate to tell you, but the second time I met Alec, he actually seemed pretty normal."

"More normal than Dash, I bet," Lauren teased. Dash and Lauren poked and tickled each other.

"Maybe we *should* write an article about Brady," said Dash. "Especially since we have an inside source."

Faith rolled her eyes. "Forget it."

Lauren leaned into Dash. "How about finishing our recycling article first?"

"You creative-writing majors," Dash teased. "You're just born realists."

"And you journalism majors," Lauren tossed back, "are born procrastinators."

Dash shrugged.

Lauren pointed to her notebook. "Come on, Dash. We'd better finish this article by tomorrow. Especially since we're going away this weekend."

"You're going away this weekend?" KC questioned.

Lauren pretended to cringe. "We're going to visit Dash's parents."

Dash put a towel over his face and pretended to be dead.

"It should be interesting." Lauren laughed.

"I'm sure it will be great," KC saïd honestly.

Dash mumbled from under the towel. "We'll let you all gossip about it next week, if we survive."

They all tipped their faces back up to the sun.

KC grabbed her tube of suntan lotion and began applying it carefully to every exposed millimeter of skin. As excited as she was about Faith's date with Alec and about Lauren's plans to spend the weekend with Dash's family, it also made her feel a little left out.

KC reminded herself that things were going well. Maybe Faith had an extraordinary Saturday night planned, but KC had a spectacular Saturday night ahead of her, too. After all, the Providence Ball wasn't exactly the same as sitting around the dorm watching reruns on TV. KC knew going to that ball with Courtney might be the most important thing she would do all freshman year. Her life was finally coming together! So she couldn't figure out why she still felt like something important was missing.

"Where's Winnie?" KC suddenly asked.

Faith looked around. "Yeah, where is Winnie? I left a note on her door telling her to meet us here."

"Winnie went downtown to meet her mother," Lauren reminded them.

"Oh, right," Faith remembered. "Her mom is giving a speech or something at the new Crisis Hotline place downtown. I forgot that was today." She squinted. "I guess I've kind of forgotten about Winnie for the last few days. I hope she's okay."

KC hadn't forgotten about Winnie. Even though she hadn't seen Winnie since Western Civ, KC thought about her all the time. When KC was planning her outfit for the charity ball or talking to Courtney about the shoot, thoughts of Winnie popped into her head. Even when she'd been racking her brains, straining to put together a decent paper about Heathcliff and *Wuthering Heights,* she kept getting distracted by worries and regrets about Winnie.

"Hey, speaking of Winnie," Lauren said suddenly. "Look who's coming over to join us."

"Who?" KC sat up, expecting to see Winnie's confused eyes and giddy smile.

But it wasn't Winnie. It was Winnie's roommate, Melissa McDormand, walking arm in arm with her boyfriend, Brooks Baldwin. In spite of all the anger between KC and Winnie lately, KC was disappointed to find that Winnie wasn't going to show up.

As Melissa and Brooks strolled closer, KC overheard Melissa reciting, "Actinium. Symbol, Ac. Atomic number, 89. Atomic weight, 227. Year discovered, 1899."

"Perfect," confirmed Brooks, who was checking the facts in Melissa's chemistry book. He wore a rugby shirt and cutoffs. His blond curls glistened in the bright sun.

Even as Melissa sat down next to Lauren, she kept reciting. "Aluminum. Symbol, Al. Atomic number, 13. Atomic weight, 26.9815. Year discovered, 1825." Her brown eyes barely connected with her friends. "Hi, everybody."

"Hi, Mel."

"Hi, Brooks."

Brooks waved to all of them. His gaze lingered for a few extra seconds on Faith.

"Hi," Faith said to him.

Brooks smiled easily and gazed back at Melissa. "That's two right answers in a row," he told Melissa. Then he closed Melissa's chem book. "Now, speaking of rowing . . ." He grinned and whipped off his shirt. "I wonder if we can use the canoes today."

Melissa laughed and made it through the next

element before reaching up and taking the rubber band out of her red hair. She shook her hair loose and stripped off her sweats to reveal a red tank suit. Then she grabbed Brooks's hands.

"Race you to the water," she dared.

"Race you to a canoe," he challenged.

She one-upped him. "Canoe-race you to the bridge."

"You're on," Brooks gloated, charging off ahead of her. Melissa took off in a sprint, quickly overtaking him.

After Melissa and Brooks had each climbed into a canoe, Faith sat up and put her chin in her hands. "It's still strange to see my high-school boyfriend with Winnie's roommate."

KC stared at them. "Melissa does everything like it's some kind of contest."

Faith laughed. "And Brooks likes to take care of people and make sure they win. They're perfect for each other. It's weird."

"It doesn't seem weird to me," KC said. "It's nice."

"I know," Faith conceded. "It is nice."

It was very nice, KC thought. And yet the fact that even steely study grind Melissa could let go and fall in love was making KC feel worse.

KC took a deep breath, rubbed more lotion on

her legs, and sighed. The warm sun baked her skin but she still couldn't relax. There was too much nagging at her: her GPA, her extra-credit paper on *Wuthering Heights,* which wasn't done and didn't seem like it was going to get done any time soon, as well as Winnie and Courtney and the Tri Betas. Trying to will herself to let go, KC lay back down on her towel and closed her eyes.

Suddenly KC thought she must have fallen asleep, because she had the sensation of a pair of strong arms under her, scooping her up against a warm, muscular chest. She felt weightless and out of breath for a moment.

"Hello, KC."

KC's eyes flapped open. She struggled away from the arms, pushed against the chest, and scrambled to her feet. That was when she realized that she was looking into Peter Dvorsky's eyes.

Peter took a step back and looked at KC. "Well, well," he said, planting his hands on his bare waist. "We meet again." His eyes traveled the length of KC's body.

KC was suddenly self-conscious, even though she knew she looked great in her black bathing suit. And in any case, she reminded herself, Peter never noticed her looks at all. She picked up her towel and threw it at him.

He caught it with one hand. "So what are you up to, KC? Taking a break? I didn't know bored beauties took breaks. I thought they spent all their time shopping and doing their nails."

KC found herself wishing that she hadn't gone to the audition. Having Peter know she'd been cast as a bored beauty was even taking the fun out of being in a Hollywood film. "I didn't know photographers took breaks," she tossed back. "I thought they spent all their time in darkrooms until they turned into vampires."

"Not at all," he teased, facing her as if they were about to begin a wrestling match. "Photographers are on the loose as much as possible, looking for beauty in every conceivable place." He lifted his arms and looked up at the sky. "And I've certainly found it here."

"Are you saying that I'm beautiful?" KC bantered, pretending to fall back in shock. "Was that a compliment from Peter Dvorsky? No, I can't believe it. It isn't possible. I must be hearing things."

He grinned. "I said the day was beautiful, KC. And since you're part of this day, maybe you're beautiful, too. I don't know." He quickly reached out and grabbed her hand.

KC struggled to get away from him, but he

pulled her in and suddenly scooped her off the ground. "Now if I saw you soaking wet, that might give me more of a clue."

"Peter!" KC began kicking and pounding on his shoulders as he started to carry her toward the pond.

"The water exposes things that you can hide on solid ground," Peter teased. "Who knows what I'll find out when I see you dripping wet?"

"No!" KC shrieked again and beat on Peter's chest. "Put me down! Peter!"

He held her more tightly as he marched closer to the pond.

No matter how hard KC pummeled him, or how wildly she scissored her legs, he kept heading toward the water, laughing his infectious laugh.

"Have a nice swim, both of you!" KC heard Faith holler from behind her.

"Watch out for sharks," yelled Lauren.

KC was about to kick again, when she felt herself being hurled into the air. She let go with one last scream.

"Peeeterrr!"

Then she shot down into the warm, deep water. Gasping for air, KC flailed to the surface just as Peter cannonballed in after her. Water washed over her. She spluttered, then ducked her head back into the pond to slick her hair away from her face.

When Peter bobbed up, grinning at her, she curved her hand, drew it fast across the water, and doused him with a two-foot spray.

He laughed and shook his head, sending drops flying back at her.

"You're crazy!" KC shouted at him.

Peter swam up to her and grabbed her around the waist, pulling her up against his bare, slick chest. "I know."

KC kicked and fought, swallowing water and slapping her hands against Peter's arms. Then he suddenly let go of her, gave a quick grin back, and began to swim away.

"You're it," he called as he stroked off with Olympic speed. "Catch me if you can!"

KC's mouth dropped open. "Peter!"

A moment later she was swimming after him with a kick and a big, strong stroke.

Eight

"**C**risis intervention demands intuition, patience, and great sensitivity," Francine Gottlieb lectured. She stood at the front of the badly lit, low-ceilinged room in downtown Springfield and pointed to a large flow chart.

The audience, which consisted of volunteers, hotline employees, and psych majors from the university, sat in folding chairs, listening quietly and taking notes. Meanwhile Winnie stood in the back, leaning against the wall with her arms crossed. She chewed grape bubble gum and looked around at the room. The hotline office

was decorated in what Winnie called "early insti-
tution." It had formerly been a clinic, so the
walls were still hospital green, the floors were
gray, and the desks were beige Formica. The windows seemed permanently coated with grime.

"This sure is a place that'd cheer you up if you
were feeling blue," Winnie mumbled.

Nonetheless, Winnie's mother was livening up
the room with her usual dazzling display. Her
hands gestured dramatically. Her voice trilled.
Her big hoop earrings and funky bracelets
gleamed more brightly than the overhead lights.

"Picking up cues from a caller is the first step,"
Winnie's mom pointed out. "There are certain
code phrases and words to be on the lookout
for."

Yeah, thought Winnie. *Maybe I should have
those words tattooed on my forehead.*

"Giving advice isn't necessary," her mother explained. "Listening is much more important than
talking."

Winnie looked down at her feet.

"Remember that," her mother insisted. "Be a
total listener. Sometimes that's all a caller needs.
Don't waste energy worrying about what you're
going to say next or else you'll miss the caller's
real message."

Winnie lifted her head again.

"You won't have body signals to go on," her mother continued. "But you will have voice pitch, volume, and tempo. You'll have to pay careful attention to what people say and how they say it. You'll have to be aware of what they don't say, too. Expect a lot of silence. You'll have to be comfortable with that."

Winnie blew a big purple bubble. When it popped, a student turned around and glared at her. Winnie had never been comfortable with silence. Her whole life had been dedicated to noise. She talked, popped gum, sang in the shower, ran with a Walkman, and even studied with the radio or television on.

Her mother had ventured out into the audience and was handing out sheets of paper. "These are some tips on how to handle specific kinds of calls, but very few calls will fall into categories. Most of the time you will have to rely on your intuition, your ears, your common sense, and your heart."

Winnie's mom walked back to the front of the room. "Thank you for inviting me here. I hope my talk has been helpful and I wish the Springfield Crisis Hotline the very best of luck in getting off the ground."

Everyone applauded. Winnie watched her mom mingle with the crowd of people who swarmed around her. She had a sudden impulse to walk out the door and disappear before her mother even knew she'd been there. But before she could make a move, her mother raised her curly head and looked right at her.

"Win!" her mother cried, and blew a kiss.

Winnie raised her hand.

The crowd surrounding Ms. Gottlieb broke up as Winnie stepped away from the wall and walked toward the front of the room. Her mother met her halfway.

"Hi, Mom," Winnie whispered. She immediately wondered what her mother would say about her purple hair.

Her mother didn't even seem to notice. She just threw her arms around Winnie. "Hi, honey. I'm so glad to see you." Then she pulled back and looked at Winnie's face.

Winnie waited for her mother to tell her how terrible she looked.

"Did you hear my talk?" her mom asked instead. "I looked for you at the beginning, but then I got so involved in what I was saying that I couldn't tell if you'd slipped in late or not."

"I heard most of it," Winnie said. "I was standing in the back."

Her mom hugged her again. "I agreed to do this only because it would be a good excuse to come and see you." She let go of Winnie and dug through her big canvas bag. "I think I've got everything, so let's get out of here."

"Okay."

Winnie's mom leaned forward and whispered, "This place is so depressing, isn't it? You'd think between the paint job and the callers, it would be the hotline volunteers who would need therapy. I hope they fix it up once they really get the hotline going."

"Me, too."

"Let's go get something to eat. Are you hungry, Win?"

Winnie shook her head.

"You're always hungry. Come on. I saw a gourmet pizza place just down the block."

Winnie's mom steered her out of the hotline office and down the sidewalk. They stopped a few doors down, in front of a small, hip-looking diner with lace curtains and red-and-white checked table clothes. Winnie's mom put on her glasses, then squinted to read the menu, which was written on a blackboard in the window.

"It says today's special pizza is goat cheese and sun-dried tomatoes," Winnie said.

"Sounds good to me," her mom said cheerfully. "Okay with you?"

"I'm not hungry," Winnie said, but her mother didn't seem to hear her.

They went into the restaurant and sat down at a small corner table. Winnie played with the salt and pepper shakers, while her mom excused herself and went off to the bathroom.

While her mother was gone, Winnie thought about how she'd been dreading and looking forward to her mother's visit at the same time. She'd been dreading it because she didn't want her mom to see what a mess she'd suddenly become. But she was looking forward to it because her mom was a therapist, after all, and perhaps could give Winnie some insight or some help.

Her mom sat down again with newly fluffed hair and redone lipstick. She folded her hands on the table and her bracelets rattled. "Okay, let me look at you."

Winnie considered crossing her eyes, but she didn't want to put her mother in a joking mood. Actually she was relieved to finally be face to face with her. At last her mother was going to say, *Why did you do that to your hair, Win? Why did you deliberately make yourself look like a freak? What's gotten into you?*

But before Winnie's mom could say anything at all, the waiter interrupted.

"One special pizza," Ms. Gottlieb ordered. "And a beer for me. Whatever you have on draft."

"I'll just have coffee," Winnie said.

Ms. Gottlieb finished the order, then looked over at her daughter. "So what's new?"

Winnie tore little bits off her napkin. "I'm going to be an extra in this movie they're shooting at school."

"How exciting!"

Winnie shrugged.

Her mother waited for Winnie to go on. When Winnie didn't say anything else, she plunged in. "Okay. So you're going to be in a movie. That's wonderful, Win. Not many girls get to be in a movie their freshman year, or any year for that matter." She laughed and waited for Winnie to laugh, too.

Winnie stared out the window.

"And how's that boy you told me about, Win? The one who lives in your dorm?"

"Josh?"

"Josh." Her mother smiled. "As I remember,

he was wonderful, funny, sensitive, and intelligent. How is he?"

"We broke up."

"I see." Her mother sighed knowingly and sat back in her chair. "So that's why you're so down."

At least her mom had noticed she was down. Winnie chewed on her fingernail, while the waiter delivered the coffee and her mother's beer.

Her mom sat back and watched her for a few moments. "Win, this is what freshman year is all about," she said, her vibrant lecture tone returning. "It's about learning and making mistakes and even having things hurt so much that you don't think you'll ever get over them. But you will. And when you do get over them, or in this case, over him, you'll be so much stronger for it. Take my word."

Winnie bit back tears.

Her mom reached out for her hand. "I know how much it hurts, Win. But believe me, Win, you will get over Josh. It will just take plenty of time."

It isn't just Josh! Winnie wanted to scream. It wasn't just KC, either. It was herself. It was the fact that she didn't know what to do with her life. She didn't know what she was doing at college or where she was supposed to go from here. She felt so lost and useless that when painful stumbling blocks such as Josh and KC came up, she didn't know how to get past them. All she knew was that she wasn't going to become a nuclear physicist or a lawyer, a computer genius, a theater director or a businesswoman just by giving things time!

Her mother's expression grew more serious as Winnie stared down into her coffee cup. Neither of them said anything else until after the pizza arrived.

"Is it something else besides Josh?" her mother ventured.

Winnie took a slice of pizza, but merely played with the soft white cheese.

Her mother seemed to have suddenly lost her appetite, too. "Winnie, we've always been honest with each other. I've always prided myself on my open relationship with you. We've always been able to talk like friends, haven't we?"

Winnie didn't answer.

"Will you answer one question for me?"

"What is it?"

"Are you experimenting with drugs, Winnie?"

Winnie rolled her eyes and huffed. "No, I'm not experimenting with drugs!"

"Good. Thank you." Her mother seemed relieved and finally began to eat. "I'm sorry I had to ask."

Gee, Winnie thought. *At least there's something my mother doesn't want me to experiment with. At least there's one thing that won't help me by making me learn from my own mistakes!*

Her mother started picking at her pizza, looking up at Winnie every few moments with a worried expression. "Win," she finally said. "Is there anything else you want to tell me? Is there anything else that you and I need to discuss?"

"Actually, there is," Winnie heard herself blurt. "I'm thinking about quitting school."

"What?" her mother gasped.

Winnie hadn't really thought about dropping out of school until just that second, but once she'd said the words, it didn't sound like such a bad idea.

Her mother had gone pale. "Have you given this serious thought? Do you know what else you would do if you dropped out of college?"

"I'll figure it out," Winnie challenged, pushing her plate away.

"You'll figure it out?"

Winnie looked right at her. "I can take care of myself."

Her mother ate silently for quite some time. When she was finally finished, she said in a very controlled voice, "Well, Winnie, I'm sure you can take care of yourself. Dropping out of school is not what I want for you. I'd like you to finish college, but it's not my life. If you really feel that school isn't for you, then it's your choice. It's a decision you'll have to make. And you'll have to live with the consequences."

Winnie wanted to scream. Even as her mother paid the check and thanked the waiter, Winnie wanted to jump up and down and yell, *Wait! No! Stop! What if the consequences are something I don't want to live with? Can't you ever tell me 'no, don't do it, I forbid you to do it'? Can't you ever make me stop and think before I plunge in and learn from my own painful stupidity? I don't want to drop out of school any more than I want Josh to be snuggling up to Sigrid, or KC to be treating me like dirt. I just want you to help me understand why I feel the way I do and what I can do to change it!*

But Winnie didn't say anything. She accompanied her mother back to the hotline office and over to her car. Then she stared blankly as her mother slid in behind the wheel, rolled up her window, and drove away.

Nine

"You in the green jacket, take a few steps back."

"You with the long hair, take off that shiny scarf. It's giving off glare."

"Tell the jocks to wait by the wardrobe trailer!"

"Where are the wackos?"

"I want all the bored beauties to wait over here!"

On Friday at seven-thirty A.M., there were five assistant directors in McClaren Plaza, giving orders through bullhorns to the crowd of students filling up the square. Everyone was just barely awake. The overcast sky shed a pearly white glow over the extras, who were being herded around in groups separated by type.

"I don't know why they have to yell at us through those megaphone things."

"I don't know why we had to get here at six. We didn't do anything at all for the first hour and a half."

"The last time I got up this early was to go bird watching with my crazy dad."

"I hate the way this weather makes my hair frizz."

"I thought movies were exciting. All we're doing is standing around."

"It's hurry up and wait, if you ask me. Hurry up and wait."

KC had been clumped together with her group of bored beauties, which included a Gamma sorority sister, a stunning senior on the diving team, a linguistics major, and two girls who had modeled for the U of S calendar. Plus Courtney, of course, who looked dignified and fresh in a light wool skirt and a hand-knit cotton sweater.

"Have you seen Faith this morning?" KC asked Courtney.

Courtney shook her head. "No."

KC hadn't seen Faith, either. Or Peter. She'd only seen Winnie for a split second, while she was being herded across the plaza with the rest of the wackos.

KC stamped her feet. "There does seem to be a lot of waiting around."

"Yes." Courtney smiled. "It's interesting to watch everyone setting up, though."

KC nodded, as technicians carted equipment across McClaren Plaza. Meanwhile assistant directors hurried through the crowd arranging the formation of the groups, while wardrobe, hairdressing, and makeup assistants bobbed in and out. They checked clothes and made sure students weren't wearing too much makeup.

"I can't wait until tomorrow night," KC said to Courtney after another twenty minutes of waiting.

"Neither can I," Courtney assured her with a smile. "Do you need to borrow anything? I can loan you a handbag or shoes or anything else you might need."

KC shook her head. She'd already borrowed Lauren's pearls and heels, and had been assured by Lauren that her charity ball outfit was just right. "Thank you, though."

"You're welcome." Courtney patiently folded her hands. "I can pick you up at your dorm tomorrow night, if you'd like."

"Oh no," KC insisted. She was amazed by Courtney's growing warmth and generosity. "That's too much trouble. I'll meet you at the Tri Beta house."

"All right." Courtney smiled. "Why don't you come over around eight? The ball starts at eight-thirty, so that should give us plenty of time."

"I'll be there."

"Good. I'm glad you're going with me."

"Me, too."

They watched the technicians again. Finally, after another hour of waiting around, a tall woman appeared, swinging over the edge of the crowd on a boom. She was holding a mega-phone, and was dressed in a cotton sweater and crisp twill slacks. She waved a clipboard over her head to get everyone's attention. KC thought she looked more like a math teacher than someone from Hollywood.

"Everyone stand still, please. *Quiet!*" the woman commanded. She waited for the crowd to settle down. "My name is Sandra and I'll be giving you instructions for this shot. We want to thank you for being here and for your coopera-tion."

Shouts of "All right" and "Hey, any time" rip-pled through the crowd.

Sandra cut off the cheers. "You will need to listen very carefully to my instructions. It looks like it might start raining any moment, so we can't waste any time. We need to get this shot while it's still dry."

The students grew quiet.

Sandra's voice echoed across the plaza. "The scene we are about to shoot comes almost at the end of the movie. It's very important. Up until now, no one in the movie believes that Martin, our hero, could possibly have devised a system to contact UFOs. The rumors have spread that he's crazy. He's even in trouble with the local police and he's on the verge of being expelled from school."

Someone from the jock group cracked, "Sounds like the story of my life." He was promptly shushed.

"This is the scene where the UFO finally appears from behind that building," Sandra said, pointing toward the Social Sciences Building. A camera crew was set up on the roof. The crew members waved down to the students.

"After the UFO appears from behind the building," Sandra went on, "it will hover over the middle of the square and all of you will stare up at it, with varying reactions."

Murmurs ran through the crowd again.

"Where are the spacemen?"

"Does she mean a real UFO?"

"There are no real UFOs, dummy. What are you, nuts?"

KC and Courtney looked at each other.

"Needless to say," Sandra explained, "there will not be a real spacecraft hovering over the square." The moans of disappointment made her laugh. "The UFO will be added later with special effects. But we will need all of you to react as if you were seeing a UFO. Each group will be assigned an assistant director to help you rehearse your specific reactions. We want you to pay attention and to use your imaginations. When everyone is ready, the filming will begin. When you hear 'Action,' you'll know we're starting to roll the film. Have fun. And relax!"

"I guess the waiting around is finally over," KC said to Courtney with an excited grin.

Courtney looked eager, too. "I guess so."

A moment later an assistant director came over to their group. He introduced himself as Garland and gave them instructions. "Now, beauties, your reactions will be different from those of any other group. From you we want boredom that turns to shock. You don't have any idea what may be inside this spaceship. And you've never seen anything like it in your lives."

The girls nodded blankly.

Garland gestured to a red sheet that had been draped over the side of the Social Science's Building. "When I say 'Action,' you will all need to look at that red marker. Let your boredom fade, then allow shock and astonishment to build, eventually turning to horror. Imagine that UFO floating off the edge of the building and hovering over your head. Really see it and react. Can you do that?"

KC and Courtney nodded. The other bored beauties giggled and shrugged.

After more waiting, and more fiddling with lights and microphones, Garland leaned into their group again. "Okay, ladies. Here's your chance at stardom. Here we go."

KC held her breath as Garland backed up, ready to conduct their reactions with his hands.

"*U and Me,* scene four hundred and twelve, take one. Bored beauties. Action," another technician announced, clapping his slate and quickly backing out of the shot.

The camera moved in and KC pushed everything out of her head except the image of a huge metallic object rising up over the Social Sciences

Building and moving toward the plaza. It took a moment to shake off her self-consciousness, but she was starting to get into it. Some of the other bored beauties were having problems, though.

"Cut!" Garland ordered. "No, no! Come on! React! Relax and use your imaginations!"

The Gamma sister giggled.

The diver looked insulted.

Garland rolled his eyes.

The man with the slate stepped in again. *"U and Me,* scene four hundred and twelve, take two. Bored beauties. Action."

They tried to imagine the UFO one more time.

"Cut!" Garland yelled. "Come on, girls. You're supposed to start out bored, not dead! And we need astonishment and horror after that, not more boredom."

KC and Courtney frowned, but the other girls started to complain.

"How are we supposed to react to nothing?"

"Yeah. There's nothing to look at up there in the sky."

"I feel dumb."

They tried the shot again. And again. And again. Soon they were on take sixteen.

Finally, out of sheer frustration, Garland told

them to take a five-minute break. That's when KC heard a voice shout from behind her. "Cut and print! That's it, wackos! Perfect! Got it on the first take!"

KC turned and saw Winnie's group jump up and slap palms with their assistant director. Apparently the wackos hadn't had any trouble making their reactions real. KC was beginning to suspect that Winnie had more imagination in one earlobe than did the bored-beauty group put together.

When Garland came back to the bored beauties with a strained expression, Courtney leaned over and whispered to KC, "We're not very good at this, are we?"

KC shrugged. "It's not an easy thing to do. I guess that's why stars like Alec Brady make so much money."

Courtney tried to laugh, but she looked disappointed. "I guess it's hard for me to be uninhibited. The wacko group did so well."

KC stared at Courtney and felt something shift inside, as if a fault line had just resettled. On the outside, Courtney had always seemed to be everything that Winnie wasn't and all that KC had always wanted to be. She was poised, refined, elegant, and perfectly groomed. But for the first time, KC began to wonder if controlling all that external perfection didn't have its price.

Garland made them try the reaction again, but it wasn't long before KC realized that their group was holding up the entire shoot. People were staring at them. KC spotted Peter Dvorsky wandering among the extras with a camera around his neck.

"Peter!"

Peter wore a baseball cap and an old sweater. He had a sexy, relaxed smile on his face. He didn't seem to see KC right away, and KC was glad. She didn't want Peter to think of her as someone who didn't even have enough imagination to act any way other than bored.

Garland was looking frazzled. As he got the beauties ready for the next take, he urged, "Don't even try and imagine a UFO this time. Just try and think about anything that would astonish you. Anything that would make you react in horror. Think about the sun falling down on your head. Think about the world ending. Whatever. I don't care. Just put something in those empty heads and let us see a reaction on your pretty faces!"

KC saw Peter step closer and she realized that he'd really been watching her all along. He cupped his hands around his mouth and yelled, "Try pretending that someone is taking your picture first thing in the morning, before you have your makeup on!"

KC and Courtney laughed, while an expression of pure horror swept the faces of the other bored beauties.

Garland thrust his fist in the air and shrieked, "Yes! Oh, that's it! Thank you, whoever you are! Now, beauties, let's try it again!"

The crowd stilled.

"Scene four hundred and twelve, take seventeen. Action!"

This time the scene came off perfectly.

"Cut and print. That's the shot."

The students shouted with joy. The shoot had lasted from seven-thirty to twelve-thirty, and everyone was exhausted. They were glad to learn that the movie company was providing all the extras with lunch. Everyone headed to the long buffet table. Peter shot some pictures for the school paper, including one of KC clowning and sticking out her tongue. KC saw Faith, who was handing out payroll forms, and Courtney wandered off by herself to study for her International Relations class.

Just before they were all about to leave the set

for the afternoon, Sandra got up on her position on the boom and spoke into her megaphone again. "Thank you all very much. Before you all leave, I would like to announce that we'll be holding an audition. We need one person to do a featured scream."

The crowd laughed.

"The student we use will get a closeup," Sandra explained. "The closeup means the camera will be just on you. And the student we use for this closeup will also get an additional seventy-five dollars in pay."

The laughter turned to jokes and cheers, but KC wasn't taking the opportunity lightly. As usual, she was almost broke. She'd just spent the last of her meager allowance on some extra books and Cliffs Notes that she thought might help bring up her grades.

"Anyone who wants to audition, form a line right here," Sandra instructed. "The rest of you can go."

About half the crowd was sticking around. KC waved goodbye to Courtney, then jumped into the line that was forming beside the boom.

Marion Becker was leading the audition and she smiled at the group. "Well, screamers, here we are. We're in UFO land again. There's no doubt now that the ship is landing in your very own backyard, so to speak, and Martin isn't around to run interference between his alien friends and the crowd. The doors of the spaceship open. What comes out of the spaceship is terrifying."

As Sandra spoke, KC tried to picture a monster-like creature emerging from the ship.

Marion Becker gestured to the first girl in line. "All right. Let's start."

Several girls were eliminated right away because they didn't have enough intensity. One boy was dismissed because he looked too much like Alec Brady. Another girl's voice didn't come out at all. Two boys dropped out before they got to the front of the line. Finally it was KC's turn.

KC screamed, imagining a grotesque creature in vivid detail.

"Eeeeeeeeeee!"

Marion Becker nodded. "Not bad, darling. Step aside and wait while we listen to some others."

KC nodded excitedly. She stepped back, tripped over a cable, and struggled to keep upright.

The audition screams continued—high screams, low screams, grunts, squeals, and bellows. Soon KC stopped listening. She began to wonder if Marion Becker even remembered that she had asked KC to stick around.

Then there came a throaty, ragged scream that pierced the air.

"Aaagggggghhhhhhhhhhhhhh!"

The scream was terrifying. It cut through KC, stabbing real fear into her heart and making chills run up and down her spine.

Technicians gasped. Marion Becker applauded. Everyone turned and stared.

As KC poked her head forward to see who the screamer was, she heard Marion Becker gushing. "Absolutely stupendous, darling. That's the best scream I've heard in a long time. You've got the closeup."

KC peered around. Finally she caught sight of the person who had made that horrifying sound. She should have known.

The screamer was Winnie.

Ten
....

Within twenty minutes Winnie was in the makeup trailer being patted, moussed, and powdered. The bright makeup lights glared in her eyes, and the barber chair felt foreign and hard.

"Relax, Winnie," said the makeup assistant. "You'll do just fine."

Winnie closed her eyes. She wasn't worried about how she was going to do on her closeup. Too many other thoughts were racing through her head, thoughts of her mother and Josh and Heathcliff—and of KC, who had walked away so quickly when it was clear that Winnie had gotten the part. Compared to figuring out her life, screaming her guts out was a breeze.

The makeup assistant removed the tissue paper from the inside of Winnie's collar and helped her out of the chair. "Okay, Winnie, you look perfect."

"Perfectly wacko," Winnie retorted.

The makeup assistant laughed.

Sandra came into the trailer and guided Winnie out. They crossed the plaza, stopping in front of a huge light that burned Winnie's eyes. The makeup girl checked Winnie's face again, brushing on some more powder. The hairdresser respiked Winnie's hair, then adjusted her earrings. The director moved in front of her, and the lighting technician called something from above her head.

When they were finally ready, a man clapped the slate and the director pointed at Winnie as a sign for her to scream.

Without holding back, Winnie screamed and screamed and screamed.

"Aaahhhhhhhhhhhh!

She screamed so long and so loud that she felt as if her insides were being ripped apart. Her whole body was starting to feel bruised.

"Win! Win!" she heard the director shouting. "You can stop now! *That's a print!*"

The director clapped Winnie on the back and grinned, while crew members crowded around her. "Thank you, Winnie. Your scream was awesome."

"Thanks," Winnie mumbled, as she wandered away from the crew. Her throat stung, and she was suddenly exhausted. Part of her wanted to keep on screaming forever, while part of her never wanted to make any sound again.

Winnie collected her carpetbag and her jacket from the makeup trailer and headed away from the plaza. The sky was gray and the wind gusted, scattering old newspapers and leaves.

Back to my studies, Winnie thought. *Back to the real world. Back to nothing.*

Winnie started to run. She raced past the old pioneer graveyard and onto the dorm green. A groundskeeper wheeling a metal cart shouted at her, "Hey! Watch out for those flowerbeds! I just planted in there."

Winnie looked down. Without realizing it, she'd stomped straight over the formal flowerbed where the words *U of S* were spelled out in red and blue pansies.

"Sorry," she said to the flowers. "I can't do anything right—except scream."

Carefully staying on the walkway, Winnie made it back to Forest Hall. She hurried through the lobby with her head down, ignoring a relay race in which runners were balancing beer cans on their heads. Without looking up, she passed Josh's door, then dug into her bag. She sorted through messy makeup, her blue-book ramblings on Heathcliff, and some old candy wrappers before coming up with her key.

She opened her door. Her room was full of junk, and yet empty. Just like her. Melissa's anatomy models stared down at the discarded running tights, paperbacks, empty Good and Plenty boxes, and incense sticks. Pale light streaked in through the window, casting gray shadows across the debris.

"Melissa!" Winnie called out, even though it was obvious that Melissa wasn't there.

Melissa was probably setting a new world record at a track meet. KC was probably over on Greek Row making the all-important connections for her business future. Faith was probably being asked to direct a new miniseries. Josh and Sigrid were probably in his room down the hall, kissing and going over their investment plans.

Winnie stood still in the middle of her room for a moment. "Maybe I should become a hermit," she muttered to the anatomy models on Melissa's tidy desk.

She kicked a pile of clothes out of her way. No matter how hard she tried, Winnie knew she couldn't stand being alone for long. She would just keep thinking about the happy moments she'd spent in Josh's room, lying in his arms, hearing him say, "I love you."

Winnie sat on her bed and wondered how she was going to make it through the evening. She began to feel the weight of real depression. It pulled at her, making her feel dark and heavy.

Finally she shot back to her feet and yanked her door open. Stereos throbbed, vibrating the floor. She was heading for the stairs, but stopped suddenly when she saw the hall phone. Hesitating, she grabbed the receiver, pushed change into the coin slot, and dialed her mother's number.

As she waited for her mother to pick up, she recalled her mom's advice: *Make your own mistakes; learn from the consequences.*

"Hello?" her mother's voice finally answered.

Winnie froze.

"Can I help you?" her mother prodded.

At the sound of her mother's voice, Winnie was suddenly speechless. She dropped the phone back into its cradle, and leaned against the wall, staring at the messages and phone numbers scratched into the paint. She shoved her hands into the pockets of her sweater.

That was when she saw it, pinned up next to a notice for used textbooks and another for a lost purse.

Need someone to talk to? the flyer said. *Need someone to listen? The Springfield Crisis Hotline is always there for you.*

With trembling hands, Winnie dug into her pockets for more loose change, and punched the hotline's number. The phone rang and rang.

"Crisis Hotline," answered a harried voice.

Winnie opened her mouth, but the hotline counselor was too quick for her.

"I'm terribly sorry," he blurted. "We're really short-handed tonight. Can you hold?"

Winnie stared at the phone as he cut her off. *"No!"* she shouted. "I can't hold!"

She didn't wait for the counselor to come back on. Instead she tore the flyer off the wall and threw it on the floor. Then she ran past Josh's door, through the lobby, and out into the night.

Winnie knew that she was running away. She

was running away from college and her dorm. She was running away from Josh and her mother, from KC and from her life.

It had begun to rain and the temperature was dropping. The wind whipped through her sweater. Winnie dodged the pools of light, staying in the pitch-black shadows until she had passed Faith's dorm, the dining commons, and Rapids Hall.

Winnie didn't stop until she passed by Langston House, the all-girls study dorm where KC lived. For some reason, Winnie wanted to make some kind of connection with KC before she ran off and never came back.

Winnie looked up. A few lights burned in the windows. She jogged up the wooden steps, punched open the carved door, and let it bang shut. The dorm was quiet and the thick carpet muffled her footsteps.

When Winnie reached KC's undecorated door, she hesitated. It wouldn't do any good to knock. Instead she reached into her bag and considered leaving KC a note.

Dear KC: I know I'm not good enough for you to be my friend anymore. So go on. Be a success. I will no longer be around to embarrass you.

But when Winnie looked at the mess of papers

in her bag, she knew that any message she could leave would be even more pathetic than this act of running away. So she pulled out the blue book in which she had written about her friends, and Heathcliff and *Wuthering Heights* instead. She ripped out the pages on Heathcliff and stuck them under the door of KC's single room.

"There," Winnie muttered quietly. "Take that, KC. Maybe it'll at least help you bring up your English comp grade. Maybe you'll remember that, just once, I did something right."

Eleven

It had rained all Friday night, but KC didn't realize it until she woke up the next day. It was almost noon. Her tiny, old dorm room smelled musty. The sound of pounding water echoed in her head.

"Oh, no," KC sighed, realizing that she had left her window open all night. The curtains were damp and there was a line of water on her desk.

"My Heathcliff paper!" KC suddenly flew out of bed. She shut her window, then made sure that the paper she was working on hadn't gotten wet.

"Thank God," she moaned, sorting through

the pages. She read aloud, " 'It is the agony of denied love that sends Heathcliff into the night.' "

It was all there. Every word of her extra-credit paper for English Composition. She'd been up until four writing it, with the help of Winnie's notes. It was still far from finished, but at least she'd made a decent start.

"Win, why did you do this for me?" KC asked aloud, as she sat at her desk chair and went right back to work.

The previous night, KC had gone to a party on Frat Row. She'd returned early, and that was when she'd found Winnie's blue book stuck under her door. At first KC had thought it was some kind of snide reminder that Winnie always got A's with nothing but late-night cramming, while she worked and strained to barely get B's and C's. But then she had flipped through the blue book and realized that it was a present. Winnie had been as generous as ever, in spite of the horrible way KC had snubbed her lately. It had made KC remember a time in high school when Winnie had been losing her mind over some guy, but had still remembered to make KC for Class President posters and tack them up all over school.

"Oh, Win."

KC reached into her desk and took out some crackers and an apple she had snuck out of the dining commons the night before. That would sustain her for the afternoon at least. She wouldn't have to leave her room until the paper was completely done.

Leafing through Winnie's frantic scrawl again, KC began to feel more and more confident. She hadn't copied Winnie's notes or conclusions. She was just using Winnie's ideas as a jumping-off point, because Winnie had found so many things in *Wuthering Heights* that KC hadn't realized were there.

KC thought and scribbled, barely noticing as the hours passed. She stopped every once in a while to watch the rain let up and then start pouring down again. She kept working, feeling a growing sense of satisfaction as the pile of notebook paper grew beside her.

It was almost five o'clock when KC finally checked her watch.

"Oh, my God!"

She pushed her chair away from the desk and got up to look at herself in the mirror.

"The Providence Ball!"

She had to be ready before eight. Her hair was

a mess and she still had to go out and buy pantyhose and some lipstick. She'd been so caught up in Heathcliff's visions and Winnie's notes that she'd completely lost track of time.

"Get moving, KC," she muttered, rummaging through her closet for her mother's old rain poncho and a hat. She had just enough time to get the bus downtown, pick up what she needed, then grab something to eat, shower, fix her hair, dress, and get over to Sorority Row.

Grabbing her purse, KC crossed to the door, yanked it open, then stopped when she realized that two people were standing on the other side.

"Hi," KC said, taking a step back and staring at Melissa and Brooks. Melissa was dressed in her U of S sweats, while Brooks wore jeans and a hiking parka. They both had wet hair and their faces were dripping with rain. "What's going on?"

"We're not sure," Melissa answered in her straightforward way. "That's why we came to talk to you."

"Oh?" KC looked from Melissa to Brooks and back again. She didn't want to seem impatient, but she needed to be on her way.

Then KC looked at Melissa more closely and stopped worrying about the time. There was something in Melissa's eyes that made KC's heart beat faster. It wasn't Melissa's usual determination or concentration. It looked more like fear.

KC gave a questioning glance to Brooks.

"KC," Melissa said, "have you seen Winnie?"

"What do you mean? I saw her yesterday at the movie shoot. But I haven't seen her since." KC looked down. "We're not exactly speaking to each other these days."

"Winnie didn't come back to her room last night," blurted Brooks.

"Are you sure?"

"I got in late," Melissa explained, "because I went to a lecture at the medical center downtown. I saw that she wasn't in her bed, but I just figured she'd gone to a party or something and I went to sleep." Melissa paused for breath. There was a deep furrow of worry between her brows.

"What about this morning?" asked KC.

Brooks put his arm around Melissa and she went on. "When I got up I could tell that she hadn't been in the room all night, so I thought maybe she'd slept in your room or in Faith's. I know how bummed out she's been lately, so I thought she might have gone to stay with her old friends."

KC swallowed hard.

"I haven't been able to find Faith," Melissa went on.

"Faith is somewhere near McClaren Plaza, putting in her last day on the movie," Brooks said. "Things are so crazy over there that it was impossible to find her."

KC nodded.

Melissa stepped into the room. "So then I thought maybe Winnie and Josh made up and she spent the night with him. But I haven't been able to find Josh, either. I did see his roommate, Mikoto, who said that there's no way Winnie and Josh are back together. As far as he knows, Josh is seeing someone else. Mikoto hasn't seen Winnie, either."

KC was starting to get a horrible, scared feeling in the pit of her stomach. "Maybe she went home to see her mom," she managed to say. "Maybe she got on the bus and went back to Jacksonville."

Brooks shook his head. "I called her mom just before we came over here. Winnie isn't in Jacksonville. Her mom is really worried about her. She said that Winnie told her she wants to drop out of school."

"What?"

"That's what Ms. Gottlieb said. KC, I'm worried, too," Brooks explained. "I know Winnie from high school, just like you do. I know how close she can get to going over the edge. And I've run into her in the dining commons over the last two weeks and seen how upset she's been. I saw the way she acted at her surprise birthday party. I think she might be in trouble."

KC felt sick. She couldn't believe that Winnie was going to drop out of school! She couldn't believe that she'd been so obsessed with Courtney and the Tri Betas that she hadn't noticed that Winnie was heading for a fall. "What should we do?"

Melissa shrugged. "I'm supposed to be leaving any minute to get a ride to St. Clair. I'm running at a meet there tomorrow."

"I was planning to go, too," said Brooks. "But I'll stick around if you need me, KC."

KC couldn't speak for a moment. All she could think of was the last time she had seen Winnie, when Winnie had let loose with that terrifying scream. Had her old friend screamed her head off to get KC's attention?

"I'm the one she needs, Brooks," KC finally said. "You go ahead with Melissa. Winnie's probably with someone else in her dorm. At least I hope she is."

Melissa took a step back and KC realized that she was in a hurry to go. "Go ahead, Melissa," KC insisted. "Go to your track meet. You, too, Brooks. I'll find Winnie. I'll clear this up."

"Are you sure?" Brooks asked.

"I'm sure. Go on. Go."

It took another moment for Melissa and Brooks to actually leave. After they were gone KC looked frantically around the room, trying to figure out where she should search for Winnie first. Then she saw her nearly finished Heathcliff paper on her desk and her black formal in the dry cleaner's bag, waiting to be worn at the charity ball.

"Courtney," KC remembered, bringing her hands to her face. She checked her watch. She had two hours to find Winnie, and then she had to be back to meet Courtney on Sorority Row.

As soon as KC ran down the steps of Langston House, thunder boomed over her head and a torrent of rain burst from the sky. With the rain pouring onto her face, KC hurried across the green.

"Isn't rain romantic, Josh?"

"What, Sigrid?"

"Nothing. Never mind. I didn't mean to distract you from our work."

Josh sighed, leaned his chin on his hands, and stared at robust, blond Sigrid. He'd turned her desk chair backward to face her bed and was sitting in it, straddling the seat. He wasn't very comfortable, but his discomfort had nothing to do with his position.

Meanwhile, Sigrid sat cross-legged on the bed, leaning towards him. The light from the desk lamp shone on her hair, which fell loosely around her shoulders. As she read through their computer printout, she smiled. Rain flicked against the window, and occasionally the wind whistled across the green.

"This is absolutely perfect, Josh," she murmured.

"Well, you did most of the work," Josh said.

"Oh, no, I didn't. You're just saying that to make me feel good." She went back to their printout.

No, Josh thought. *I'm saying it because it's true.* Sigrid had invited him over to her dorm room in Emerald Hall, so they could put the finishing touches on their programming project. So far, she had done most of the work while he had merely stared at the walls.

He stretched his arms over his head and looked out at the rain. He was in yo-yo mode lately: up and down, up and down. Sigrid had caught him in a down swing, but even so, he didn't know why he'd agreed to go over to her room. Maybe he wanted to give Sigrid the biggest possible chance. The only thing he knew for sure was that he didn't want to spend another Saturday night thinking about how much he loved and missed Winnie.

Josh picked up a pen and clicked it. As the point popped in and out, he stared at the wall above Sigrid's desk. A calendar hung there with every square written in. *Write history paper, call home, go to aerobics, finish goal setting* . . . Little stars and checks appeared beside some of the squares. Things done well, he thought. Things done at all. He resisted the urge to flip through her calendar and check the next six months. He wondered if his own name would be written in one of those little squares.

The bedsprings squeaked. Sigrid said something, but Josh didn't really hear her. Through the blankness that surrounded him, only part of her sentence came through. ". . . and I'm so glad we had the opportunity to work . . . and get to know each . . ."

Before Josh knew what was happening, she'd crawled across the bed, gently removed the pen from his hand, and put her arms around his neck. The chair was still between them, but Sigrid was making up for the barrier with the intensity of her mouth. Josh found himself thinking that most guys would envy him. He also thought that he should probably be feeling something. He wove his fingers through her blond hair and kissed her back. He went through all the motions. But kissing wasn't something he could work at. The more he tried, the more he felt as if he'd been turned to stone.

Sigrid pulled back. "Josh?"

He blinked.

"Is something wrong?"

Her blue eyes were locked onto him and he tried to focus on her. She was attractive, bright, determined, and helpful. He smelled her heavy perfume and watched the way the light filtered through her hair.

But it was no use. He sat back and rested his forehead on the backs of his hands. "I'm sorry," he said.

"Sorry for what?"

"I don't know. For being here. For making you think I might be interested in this."

"In what?" Her voice had begun to sound defensive and pinched.

Josh gave her a weak smile. "You're a really nice person, Sigrid. It has nothing to do with you, really." He swallowed. "I just don't think I'm the person you want to get involved with."

She went pale, and all the eagerness drained from her face. "Why not?"

He took a deep breath. "Because I'm only half here these days."

She looked puzzled.

"Because I'm in love with someone else."

Sigrid's mouth dropped open. A moment later she got up from the bed. She was trying to act cool, but her face looked hard and angry. "You might have given me a hint a little sooner," she spat out.

Josh stood up, too. "I didn't know. I didn't realize what was really going on. I'm sorry."

Sigrid marched over to her window and refused to look back at him. "Nothing was going on, Josh," she said nastily. "We were just working on a project together. That's all it was. And I never wanted it to be anything more."

Josh crossed to the door. "Of course," he said, going along with Sigrid's face-saving act. He looked back at her, but she was still staring out the window with her arms crossed. "You're right. There was never a possibility of anything going on between us. We were just lab partners the whole time."

Sigrid flung back her hair.

"So now that we're done," Josh continued, pausing in her doorway, "we can just go back to seeing each other in class and saying hello and knowing there's nothing more to it than that."

When Sigrid ignored him, Josh mumbled goodbye and bolted down the hall.

He barely heard the Saturday-night laughter and the music as he ran past open doors and out into the rain. The water was really coming down and he avoided big puddles as he crossed the dorm parking lot. Even before he could see his dorm, he heard the rock music twanging and thumping away. A few minutes later he saw bodies gesturing and dancing in the lobby, so he went around to the back door and sneaked toward his room.

But Josh didn't stop at his own door. Instead he shivered and kept going until he found himself in front of number 152, Winnie's room. He dripped water on the floor and raised his hand to knock.

"Win," he whispered.

No answer.

"Melissa," he called more loudly.

Nothing.

He headed back to his own room, but before he got there he kicked an empty beer can out from under his foot. Then he bent down to pick it up and gather a crumpled piece of paper at the same time.

Crisis Hotline, the paper said in bold black letters. *Need someone to talk to?*

Josh stared at the flyer for a few seconds. His brain felt fuzzy. He'd never been the kind of person to call a hotline or ask for help. He'd always been independent and steady.

And yet his fingers were reaching into his pocket for change and he still held onto the crumpled paper. He punched the hotline number, suspecting that he would only hang up as soon as someone answered. The phone rang and rang.

Deciding that calling had been the world's worst idea, Josh dropped the phone. He went back to his room and sat on his bed, staring at the open bottle of aftershave and the rejected shirt that Mikoto had left out before going on his early date.

"Win."

Josh pulled his knees up under his chin, crossed his arms, and dropped his head onto his forearms. When the tears began to fall, he didn't try to stop them, but let them drip until his cuffs were wet.

Finally, when he couldn't stand it anymore, Josh got up and grabbed his jacket. He flipped through his collection of floppy disks, picking out the most addictive and engaging computer games.

He left Forest Hall, deciding that the only company he was fit for that night was the flickering light on a computer screen.

Twelve

....

Chicken wings. Croissants. Pâté. Pesto. Stuffed mushrooms. Chocolate truffles. Raspberry torte.

Faith stared down at the wrap-party buffet, trying to decide whether the food was really meant to be eaten. Like most everything else that had happened during the shooting of *U and Me*, it all looked too perfect to be real.

"Try the plain old roast beef," said Peter Dvorsky, who stood next to her with his camera slung around his neck. He had a thin slice of meat on his fork and was munching on it. "It's the best thing here."

Faith leaned down and tasted some. "Mmm. You're right."

"The simplest things are usually the best." Peter grinned. "Cheers." He nudged Faith's shoulder, then went off to try and get a few more pictures before heading back to the dorms.

Faith had no desire to dine and dash. First of all, Alec hadn't arrived yet. Since it had rained all day, his final shooting schedule had been delayed. He wouldn't be meeting her at the wrap party until at least seven. Besides, the private salon in The Blue Whale, the best restaurant in Springfield, was beautiful. Arrangements of fresh flowers sat in every corner. A jazz quartet played upbeat music, blocking out the noise of the storm outside. And talkative, sunny-faced movie folk glided around, making the room look even more spectacular.

"I thought we'd never get that take right in front of the library," said the sound technician.

"We didn't," confirmed his assistant. "But we can probably fix it later in looping."

Faith smiled at them and began to wander around, not feeling at all out of place. That afternoon Merideth, Faith's buddy from the theater-arts department, had arranged for her to borrow an antique blue velvet dress from the University

Theater's costume stock. And before going off for her weekend with Dash, Lauren had loaned Faith a slim gold bracelet and her very best pumps. Faith knew she couldn't compete with the designer dresses or the Hollywood chic, but she felt comfortable. She felt pretty.

She continued to wander, sipping mineral water and listening to conversations.

"So I called my agent as soon as I finished this afternoon," Elizabeth Seymour was telling the head costumer. "I told her I'm out of work again, and she'd better find me something and she'd better find it fast."

Faith moved on, waving to Marion Becker, who was laughing with one of the assistant directors. Marion waved back, and Faith squeezed past the bar and behind Fred Gorman, the director.

"Now we only have three more months of postproduction ahead of us," Fred was complaining to the producer.

"We'd better be done in three months," the producer tossed back.

Fred groaned and held his head.

The party got more and more crowded as the minutes passed. Faith continued to roam until someone stepped in front of her to greet a new arrival and Faith was pushed backward into a potted palm. She lost her balance and started to slip. Just then a hand shot out and grabbed her elbow, supporting her weight until she steadied herself.

"Thank you," she gasped.

"No problem. You're just the girl I was looking for. Have you been waiting long?"

"No, not too long. But I'm glad you're here."

"I'm glad I'm here, too."

Faith smiled.

It was Alec Brady.

KC was running across the U of S athletic field. Rain clattered on the bleachers and the wind made the trees sway. She clutched at her mother's old poncho and shielded her eyes.

"Winnie!" she yelled as loudly as she could.

There was no answer. KC had already checked the gym, asking the three solitary basketball players if they'd seen anyone who looked like Winnie. She'd checked the indoor running track and the weight room. She'd even checked the sauna and the pool. Finally she'd gone out in the rain again, dashing back across the soggy grass.

She put her head down as she ran into the wind, hurrying toward the student union. As she banged in through the doors, she saw that the building was almost deserted. About a dozen students loitered in the snack bar, and only two sat in the TV lounge.

KC stopped a janitor who was mopping the floors, but he shook his head. "I don't remember seeing anyone with purple hair. But there's the upstairs with the balcony and the study lounges."

KC hurried up the stairs, but all the rooms that weren't locked were empty. She made one more trip through the bathrooms and the game room before leaving the building.

"Maybe she's back in her room by now," KC said to herself, as she ran back past the pioneer graveyard and across the green. She could feel her hair frizzing and prayed that she would still have time to wash it before the charity ball.

KC checked her watch as she ran up the steps to Forest Hall. It was almost seven-thirty. She ignored the lobby party, cutting quickly through the crowd and making it to Winnie's floor. She knocked loudly on Winnie's door. Then she scooted down the hall to Josh's door and pounded on it. No answer there, either. She puffed out a huge breath, then ran down to the basement. The laundry room and the study room were empty, too.

"Oh, Winnie."

KC didn't know where else to look. Winnie had been missing for almost twenty-four hours. And KC had exactly one hour to get herself dressed and over to Sorority Row.

"Where are you?"

Finally KC went back to Langston House and headed for the shower. She didn't know what else to do. All she knew was that both she and Winnie were running out of time.

"How's the party?" Alec asked Faith after he'd gotten some food and found them a fairly quiet corner.

"Great," she said. "I mean, I don't exactly go to parties like this very often. It's wonderful. It's exciting."

He smiled and Faith suddenly felt self-conscious again, as if she no longer knew what to say. She hadn't seen much of Alec since their talk in the political-science office. He was wearing an expensive-looking sportcoat and scarf with worn blue jeans. He really looked like a movie star this time. She wondered if he regretted asking her to be his date. She tried to think of something to say as the music grew louder.

"Sorry?" Alec asked in a loud voice. "Did you say something?"

Faith shook her head. "No. Did you?"

"No." He went back to his plate.

"So how was your last day of filming?" Faith finally asked.

"Okay," he answered blandly. "It's over. I go home tomorrow and then it's on to the next film."

"Well, at least you get to say goodbye to everybody at this party," Faith rambled, trying to keep some kind of conversation going.

He shrugged. "These things are always pretty predictable. The technical people relive horror stories, the actors relive golden moments, the producers count up costs."

Faith nodded, as if she understood his point.

They stood there a little longer, bobbing slightly to the music. Meanwhile a few of the cast members and some of the college helpers began to dance.

Faith mouthed the words to the song and tapped her thigh. She knew that Alec was bored, but she wasn't sure what she was supposed to do about it. Then she saw something that surprised her even more than Alec's boredom. Someone was at the doorway of the room, craning her neck and arguing with the woman who checked the invitation list. Other guests near the door were starting to gossip and stare.

It took a moment for Faith to realize that the person at the door was KC!

"That's my friend," Faith pointed out. "The one in the long black dress."

Alec looked over, his eyes brightening with interest. "One of your old friends? The ones you told me about?"

Faith nodded.

"It looks like she's trying to get into the party."

Faith started to move, but Alec was ahead of her. "I'll handle it," he promised. "You stay here."

Members of the crew and other cast members tried to waylay Alec, as he made his way through the crowd and over to the door, but he pushed past them. When he came back, he had KC with him.

"KC," Faith gasped.

KC had a wild, terrified expression. She was wearing the black dress she'd bought for Winter Formal and clunky rubber rain boots. She carried her mother's plastic poncho, a clear plastic rain bonnet, and a big red-and-white tote that Faith guessed contained makeup and shoes. Drops of water dripped from her rain bonnet and poncho.

"Thank you for getting me in," KC blurted to Alec. She didn't linger on him. She turned immediately to Faith. "Faith, I don't know what to do! I have to get back to Sorority Row to meet Courtney and I still haven't found Winnie."

"Why do you need to find Winnie?" Faith asked.

"She's been missing since last night," KC ranted. She shook the rain off wet hands and shivered. "Melissa said she never came home. I've called and walked and searched everywhere I could think of on campus and I don't know where she is. She didn't go home to Jacksonville and she's not with Josh. I'm really afraid that something terrible has happened."

Faith panicked. "She's been missing since yesterday?"

"Unless you've seen her," KC said hopefully. "Have you? Has Winnie been with you?"

Faith shook her head. "I haven't seen Winnie since the shoot Friday." She felt a deep pang of guilt. "I guess I've barely even thought about her since then." She suddenly realized that Alec was watching her and KC with great interest.

KC took a step back. "Listen," she said to both of them, "I'm sorry for ruining your party like this, but I had to tell you. I don't know what to do. I'm supposed to be at this charity ball and I have to leave right now." KC looked around. "So I guess I'll go," she continued frantically. "I guess there's nothing I can do but meet Courtney and go."

Faith nodded.

KC didn't budge. "I mean, Courtney's waiting for me, after all. And those tickets cost a fortune, so I'd really better get going. I just wanted you to know."

Suddenly Alec stepped forward. "Go on," he told KC. "Go to your party." He put his hand on Faith's shoulder. "Faith and I will leave right now. We'll drive around town and see if we can find out anything about your friend."

Faith looked over at him, astonished. "What about this party?"

"I told you," he bantered, the dimples appearing on his cheeks, "I've never liked these parties. I'd rather spend the evening looking for your lost friend."

Faith looked at KC, then back at Alec. "But all these people will wonder where you've gone.

And you don't even know Winnie. This isn't something you need to worry about."

"I'm sick of these people, Faith," Alec said. "I *want* to help you look for your friend."

He put his arm through hers and began to walk her toward the door. KC accompanied them as Alec picked up his raincoat and Faith got her raincoat. Then Alec evaded Fred Gorman and the producer and all three of them slipped out of The Blue Whale.

They waited under an awning while the attendant went for Alec's car. The rain was coming down in sheets again, making such a racket that it was hard to talk.

"Where do you want me to drop you, KC?" Alec finally asked, after his rented Mercedes had been delivered and they had climbed in.

"She needs to go to the Tri Beta sorority house," Faith said. "I'll tell you how to get there."

"Okay."

They drove through the dark rain for ten minutes until they neared Sorority Row.

But as soon as Alec changed lanes to make the turn, KC leaned forward in the back seat.

"I can't get out here," KC said.

Faith turned around and stared at her.

KC stared back. "I'll call and tell Courtney I can't go. I'll tell her I'm sorry, but there's something much, much more important that I have to do."

Thirteen

Winnie had been staring at the downtown pavement for hours. The soles of her feet burned and the back of her neck was sore. Her wet hair drooped into her eyes, and her sweater was soaked with rain.

She'd spent the previous night in the Greyhound bus station, watching the television that hung suspended on the wall and listening to the storm beat the side of the building. Buses had come and gone. Travelers had arrived and departed. She'd slept a little, but mostly she'd just sat. Finally, at five A.M., the new ticket seller had come on and chased her out.

"Hey, beat it, kid" he'd yelled at her. "Do you think this is a hotel or something?"

After that, Winnie had wandered out into the early morning. She'd walked from one end of Springfield to the other. She'd wandered through grocery and department stores and across Mountain Street Park. She'd spent hours in the downtown library. When the storm was at its worst, she happened to be sitting in the bleachers of the Springfield High School football field. Before she'd found the energy to move, she'd gotten completely soaked.

Since sundown she'd been trudging along the pavement again, scarcely noticing when the cars sped past, splattering her with water and mud. She felt numb all over. When she jammed her hands into the pockets of her jeans her fingers barely felt the coins. Yet she didn't have to feel the coins to know what was there—seventy-five cents. That was all she had left.

At the corner of Oak and Second, Winnie ducked into a coffee shop that had hanging lights and a long counter with a big clock hanging over it. It was eight-thirty. Winnie almost started to cry, as she headed for a big, plush booth. She

wanted to stretch out on the plump seat and go
to sleep. She knew that if she didn't get some real
sleep soon, she would lose what little strength
she had left. And yet she couldn't get herself to
go back to her dorm room.

A waitress glared down at her. "What can I get
you?" she drawled.

"Coffee."

"What else?"

Winnie thought back to her seventy-five cents.
"Nothing else."

"Honey, you just want coffee, you got to sit at
the counter. I need the booth for larger parties."

Winnie glanced around the restaurant. Two
men lounged at the counter, leaning forward on
the red vinyl stools.

"But there's no one else here but those guys,"
Winnie pointed out.

The waitress put her hand on her hip. "I told
you, I don't serve singles in booths."

"Forget it." Winnie stood up and ran out the
door. As she stepped outside, she felt the waitress
staring at her and looked back to see the woman
standing in the doorway, watching her with
folded arms and a disgusted sneer.

Winnie hurried down the sidewalk. The wind
howled, and the rain started again, drumming on

the parked cars and trickling down her face. Winnie tramped past darkened storefronts, junk shops, parking lots, rooming houses, and car dealerships. Now and then someone passed her, but no one paid any attention.

Finally Winnie reached the north end of Springfield, where the dingy warehouses were replaced with posh hotels, designer shops, chic cafés, and jewelry stores. Winnie spotted an awning and an open door. She dashed up the carpeted steps and stepped into the lobby of the Grandview Hotel. Quickly, she cut to the side of the lobby and sank down in an overstuffed chair. The dampness of her clothes seeped into her skin and she shivered.

Murmuring voices sounded from the hotel restaurant, and the faint sound of a string quartet drifted across the lobby. The chair she sat in was soft, deep, and comfortable. She let out a long sigh. She closed her eyes and started to drift off.

A tap on her shoulder woke her up.

"Excuse me, young lady."

Winnie squinted. A man wearing a dark blue uniform decorated with gold braid and shiny buttons was looming over her. His eyebrows were knitted with concern and his voice was soft and kind. "I'm terribly sorry, but I can't allow you to sleep here," he said.

Winnie couldn't get her body to move.

"There is a no-loitering policy," he explained with sympathy. "I know the weather outside is terrible, but if you don't leave voluntarily, I'm afraid I'll have to call the police."

Winnie breathed in, and another shiver ran down her back. Without saying a word, she stood up and walked out the lobby door.

She walked and walked and her tears began to pour down, mixing with the misty rain. *Okay, world!* she felt like screaming. *I got your message. There's nothing I can do and nowhere I can go. I'm getting the signal, loud and clear.*

Winnie headed southward again and soon the streets matched her mood. Litter clogged corners and cats skittered into alleyways. Dirty water gushed into the storm drains. An empty ache growled in Winnie's stomach. She couldn't remember when she'd eaten last. She remembered sticking her *Wuthering Heights* notes under KC's door but couldn't remember how long ago it had been. Thinking about KC again made Winnie feel even emptier. She didn't know why she wanted to hang on to KC. KC certainly hadn't wanted to hang on to her. Why couldn't she be like KC and just let go?

When Winnie walked past the darkened doorway of a used-furniture store, she was only half conscious of a hissed whispering behind her. She crossed an empty street and stepped up onto a curb. Then she became aware that someone was following her. Someone was getting close. She heard the distinct rustle of clothing. She heard footsteps and felt someone put a hand on the back of her hair.

She tensed.

"Hey, baby," the voice said.

Winnie sped up. She couldn't think anymore. She couldn't speak.

The man crossed in front of her. He was middle-aged and unshaven and he reeked of tobacco. Winnie tried to dodge him, but he stayed right at her elbow. When he reached for her again, Winnie froze. She thought back to her famous scream, took a deep breath, and planted her feet on the ground. But this time not a sound came out of her mouth, as her eyes widened with fear . . .

At the Providence Ball, Courtney Conner's most polite and elegant smile was firmly in place.

She smiled at the frilly tables, at the dance band, and at all the well-dressed people finding their place cards and sitting down to dine. She remembered her mother telling her, "Don't ever let anyone know when you're bored, or people will think that you are boring as well."

As Courtney listened to the overdressed woman on her right, however, she wondered if she cared what Mrs. Sebastian Evers thought of her. All Courtney knew was that boredom was creeping up her body like paralysis. She sipped her grapefruit juice and tried very hard to pay attention to what her tablemate was saying.

"And, of course, with all those film people running all over town, we were lucky to get a limousine at all," Mrs. Evers went on.

Courtney's smile faltered. She wished the waiters would hurry up. The auction was over, and a late supper was about to be served. Her only hope was that Mrs. Evers would be too polite to talk while she was eating.

"Those film people," Mrs. Evers continued to complain. "On Wednesday they closed down the entire shopping area on The Strand just for their silly movie. The traffic was backed up all the way to Dunkirk Bridge."

Courtney shrugged.

"And last night they shut down my favorite restaurant, just so they could use it in a shot," Mrs. Evers said.

Courtney thought of defending the movie company. All they had done was to bring something different to Springfield. And they'd asked her to imagine something that wasn't there. Courtney knew she must have learned something from that experience, because she wasn't having any trouble imagining what a good time she might have had that evening with KC.

Mrs. Evers's small eyes studied Courtney's dress. "That gown is a Rossetti, isn't it?"

"Yes, it is."

"Well, you certainly have the figure to pull it off."

"Thank you." Courtney knew the gown looked good on her. With a fitted bodice and full skirt, it was perfect for dancing, although Courtney hadn't spotted anyone she particularly wanted to dance with. She knew the gown made her look elegant and classy. And yet she had a crazy yearning to change into a Day-Glo crop top and a pair of sequined tights.

"Where's your friend tonight, Miss Conner?" Mrs. Evers asked, referring to the empty seat on Courtney's left.

"Well . . ." When Courtney had gotten KC's message, she was surprised at the wrenching disappointment she'd felt. "My guest had an emergency."

"Oh? Nothing serious, I hope."

"I hope not." Courtney had no idea what had happened. The message had just said that KC wouldn't be able to make it and that something very important had come up. Courtney prayed that she hadn't been wrong about KC and that KC hadn't intentionally stood her up. After defending KC and kicking Marielle out of the sorority, Courtney had to believe that KC was worthy of her loyalty.

A faint grimace crossed Mrs. Evers's face. "Well, I hope your friend is all right."

"So do I."

The waiter finally arrived with the soup. He tried to flirt with Courtney as he served. Courtney sat back, trying to ignore his leers and hoping that he didn't dump the tomato bisque into her lap.

The chandeliers glittered overhead, sending specks of reflected light onto the crystal and china in front of her. A string quartet played Mozart in the corner, and quiet voices murmured as the dinner began.

Courtney silently ate her soup, listening to the clink of goblets and the clatter of sterling. As the pork loin replaced the soup, a terrifying thought came to her. If she weren't careful, she'd end up like Mrs. Evers. She'd be attending charity events just so she could wear her diamonds.

Courtney sighed. It was going to be a long evening.

"What are we going to do?" KC shouted.

It was still raining. KC's long black formal had soaked up water from puddles on the sidewalks. The dampness reached her knees.

"Don't panic, KC," Faith said, sounding as frantic as KC. "Please, don't panic."

"Faith is right," said Alec. "We won't do your friend any good if we totally flip out."

They were standing at the corner of Bartlett Street and University Avenue, about three blocks from campus. Water surged down the gutters carrying with it trash and topsoil. Alec had an umbrella, but the wind had turned it inside out. All three of them were drenched and very cold.

"Let's at least get under the bus stop," shouted Alec, and they ran toward the glass-covered bench. Standing under the shelter, they wiped the water off their faces.

KC hugged her arms to her chest. "I can't stand the thought that Winnie might be out in this rain somewhere. Oh, please let her be indoors, somewhere warm and safe. Please." She was bouncing up and down, partly to try to keep warm, partly in nervous agitation.

Faith patted her. "I don't know where else we can look, KC. We checked the Zero Bagel and the Beanery. We checked Luigi's and the other college hangouts. Where else can we go?"

"What if she left town?" KC cried. "You know how impulsive she is. What if she decided to quit school on Friday and is never coming back here again?" Tears filled her eyes, and her chin began to quiver.

"KC, don't worry." Faith gave her friend a long hug. Then she pulled back and looked into KC's eyes. "I've never seen you like this."

"I've never had one of my best friends disappear before!" KC shrieked.

Faith took a step back. "I don't think Winnie felt like your best friend the last few weeks."

"I know," KC moaned. "This is all my fault."

"No." Faith sighed. "It's all of our faults. Yours, mine, and Winnie's."

They stood staring at the street, while Alec tried to shield them with his broken umbrella.

Finally he said, "Maybe we're being too logical just thinking of the places she used to go. Maybe we should try to think of some off-the-wall places. From what you've told me about Winnie, she might be anywhere."

Faith broke away from KC and stared at Alec. "I can't believe you're sticking with us. Why in the world would you, a movie star, want to run around in the pouring rain, looking for somebody you don't even know?"

Alec looked at Faith and smiled. "Just crazy, I guess." Then he rubbed more water off his face and added with concern, "I want to help. And I wouldn't blame myself if I were you. To me this is a pretty impressive show of friendship."

Faith looked back at him. Then she turned away and said, "Listen, KC, Alec is right. Maybe we're looking in the wrong places. Far-out places are always a possibility with Winnie."

KC stuck her hands under her rain poncho. The wind whipped around the corner of the bus stop, and her dress flapped. "I know. But I still think she's somewhere familiar, someplace where all of us used to go." She raised a fist and let out a groan of frustration. "Look, we're not doing any good just standing here. At least we should keep looking somewhere."

When neither Alec nor Faith had a suggestion, KC blurted, "Well, I think we should split up. We'll cover more ground. Faith, we can meet back at your room at midnight."

Alec looked skeptical.

"You two go together," KC insisted. "Get in the car and cover the streets again. I want to head back toward campus and check the hangouts one more time."

"We can all stay together and use my car," Alec offered.

"I can call a cab if I need to," KC insisted. "I just have this feeling that if I really think about Winnie and go by myself, I might actually find her."

"KC, are you sure?"

KC was already backing down the street. "You two cover all the downtown streets again. Just drive up and down and around as many times as you can before midnight. Then we'll meet again in Coleridge Hall."

Alec and Faith looked at each other, then made a run for Alec's car.

KC stood in the rain until their footsteps had faded away. Then she began to walk back toward the campus with her arms wrapped around her chest and her eyes open. When she passed Sorority Row she saw the lights of the Tri Beta house and cringed.

Sorority Row was the one place KC knew not to look for Winnie. And it was the one place that KC had always wanted to be.

"Please be all right, Winnie." KC whispered as she closed her eyes and walked past the big Greek houses. "If you're all right, I'll never do anything to hurt you again."

Fourteen

••••••••••••••••••••••••••••••••••

Winnie was running.

Her voice might not have responded, but at least her legs had taken over. She charged down the dark, wet streets. She ran through the rain—and ran and ran and ran.

At first, heavy footsteps followed close behind her. "Hey, get back here!" But soon Winnie heard gasping breath, coughing, then nothing but her own thoughts. Nonetheless, she kept running, pumping her legs and arms until her muscles burned and the sweat poured down her back.

She squeezed her eyes together to clear her vision. The lights shimmered in the wet air. In the dampness, street lamps and stoplights and flickering neon signs all blurred together. She kept racing, feeling like Melissa at the track meet of her life. Once she slid on the slick pavement, but she ran on, away from the run-down buildings and into a business section of Springfield that looked faintly familiar.

When she was finally sure that no one else was around, she slowed down. Small offices and neat shops lined the street. Near the center of a block of brick buildings, light leaked out from two large windows. Winnie wrinkled her forehead as she drew closer to the windows, which were topped by a painted sign lit by spotlights that flickered as if they were about to go out.

Crisis Hotline, the sign said. *Help When You Need It.*

Winnie staggered to a stop and almost started to laugh. "Help when I need it?" she mocked. She flopped over her knees to catch her breath and felt the rain fall on her back.

Her fear suddenly flipped over into a blaze of anger. She took a deep breath to slow her pounding heart, pulled back her shoulders, and strode to the door of the hotline office. If nothing else, she could tell the hotline people what a lousy job they were doing.

Winnie was still breathing hard, the sweat and rain dripping down the back of her neck, when she walked into the building and felt the blast of dry heat. The lights in the office were bright. There were the distinct sounds of two voices, one male and one female.

Winnie walked in further, recognizing the dreary institutional green walls and the grubby floor.

Two people sat in the big room, even though there were six or seven desks. One was Teresa Grey, the graduate student who had introduced Winnie's mother when she'd given her lecture. The other was a blond young man with tired eyes. They were both wearing jeans and sweat-shirts, and held telephone receivers in their hands.

Winnie stood there shivering, but they didn't notice her. Teresa and the man were too busy with their callers. Both were hunched over their desks, listening and jotting down notes. They wore similar expressions of patience and concern.

Finally Winnie slumped down in an office chair. Eventually Teresa looked up from her telephone and stared. Winnie didn't say anything, but Teresa held up one hand, as if to say "please wait," then went back to her call. Winnie waited, momentarily pacified because at least she was inside. But then the phone on the desk nearest her began to ring and Winnie's anger bubbled up again.

Teresa reacted to the new call, too. She pounded her desk in frustration while managing to keep her voice calm. "Can you hold on for one second?" she asked her caller in an even voice. "I have to pick up another call because we're so short-handed. Please don't hang up. I've heard everything you said. I want to keep talking to you. I promise, I'll be right back."

As soon as Teresa punched the hold button, she thrust the receiver in the air and ranted with open frustration. "I can't stand this, David! It's disgusting to keep putting people on hold like this. We might as well not even be here at all!"

The young man merely shrugged, clearly not wanting to take his attention away from his call.

Teresa shook her head and furiously punched the phone buttons. As soon as she spoke again, though, her voice sounded controlled and even. "Crisis Hotline. I'm sorry, but can you please hold? I really want to talk to you, but I'm on another call and we're terribly understaffed. I'll be back with you just as soon as I can. Please, please hang on."

Teresa went back to her first call while the new caller turned into a blinking red light on the hold button. Winnie stared at it.

"I'm listening," Winnie heard David say to his caller. "Yes. Tell me more about what happened then."

Blink. Blink. Blink.

"I understand," Teresa was saying into her telephone. "Have you thought about trying to find your own place to live?"

Blink. Blink. Blink.

Winnie couldn't stand it any longer. She saw her hand move and the next thing she knew, she had scooted up to the desk and grabbed the phone. She put the receiver to her ear and punched the hold button out of its misery.

"Hello," Winnie said in a weary tone. "Is anyone still here?"

Silence.

Winnie was about to hang up when a weak female voice on the other end of the line said, "I'm still here. Where were you?"

"I was here," Winnie mumbled. "I was here."

"Is this still the hotline?" the girl on the other

end of the line asked. Her voice cracked. "You don't sound the same."

"I'm not the same," Winnie rambled, pushing her wet bangs off her forehead. "I mean, I'm a different person than the one who first picked up your call."

"That's what I thought."

Suddenly Winnie looked up and saw that both Teresa and David were staring at her.

David stood up and put his hand over the mouthpiece of his phone. "What do you think you're doing!" he demanded in a hushed but furious voice.

Winnie didn't answer.

Teresa motioned for Winnie to put the phone back down. But before either hotline worker could do anything else, they were forced to go back to their calls.

Winnie almost put the phone back on its cradle, but then she heard the weak, weepy voice again.

"Don't put me on hold again," the girl begged. She broke into a full sob.

"I won't put you on hold," Winnie heard herself say. She glanced up briefly, but for some reason, Teresa and David's anger just ignited her own fury. Somebody had to talk to the girl, even if it was only crazy, messed-up Winnie. Winnie went back to the phone.

"Do I have to tell you my name?" the caller asked.

"Um, I don't know. Do you want to tell me your name?" Winnie improvised.

"It's okay, I guess," she answered haltingly. "My name is Janice. And . . ." She broke down again. "Well . . . oh . . . I just got fired from my job."

"Oh no," Winnie moaned.

"I was trying so hard," Janice rushed on. "I'm only just out of high school and this was my first job. I was working as a secretary for this insurance office and I thought everything was going just fine." She stopped to catch her breath.

"What happened?"

"I'm not sure. I've only been there for two weeks and yesterday they told me that they didn't think I was right for the job after all, and that they had to let me go. I know they really think I'm stupid and that I can't do the work. I don't know what I'm going to do. I also broke up with my boyfriend about a week ago and I don't have any money now and I feel like everything in my life is falling apart."

"Sounds familiar," Winnie whispered.

"What am I going to do?" Janice pleaded. "I'm totally alone now. My boyfriend left town because he wants to go to college in California and suddenly he doesn't want to be tied down. How could he do that to me? And now I lost my job. What if no one else will ever hire me? What if I get fired from every job I ever get? Sometimes I feel like Brian left me just to prove that I would fall apart without him. I think he waited until we were here and on our own, just so he could desert me and prove how dumb I am. I know I'm not smart enough for college. I don't know what I'm supposed to do!"

"What makes you think that all the kids in college are so smart?" Winnie asked.

There was a pause. "Aren't they?"

Winnie couldn't help emitting a tiny, sad laugh. "Some are and some aren't. And some are smart and really dumb at the same time."

Janice paused. "Anyway," she began again, sounding a little calmer. "See, I moved here right after high school with Brian—which my parents didn't like at all—but I told them and everyone back home how I had this great job and I was going to make it, and how Brian and I were in love and everything . . ." She started to cry again. "And now I have to call my parents and ask for money and tell them that Brian left me almost as soon as we got here and that I'm just a stupid failure after all!"

"Listen," Winnie said, "I'm no expert on mental health, but I can tell you that messing up on one job isn't the end of your life. It's only your first job. If you're anything like me, you'll go on to mess up things that are a lot more important than that."

"What?"

"Well, I don't mean that you're going to be like me. I just mean that in a while you'll look back on this and you'll be glad you don't have to work in that insurance office any more."

"Really?"

"Maybe it just wasn't the right job for you. And maybe you'll even be able to say the same thing about Brian."

Janice sniffed. "You think so?"

"I do."

There was the sound of Janice blowing her nose. "I don't know. In some ways, Brian was kind of a jerk. He was always telling me how dumb I was and that I could never do anything right."

"He sounds like a real charmer." Winnie

glanced up. Teresa had finished with her call and was walking over.

"So what do I do?" Janice wailed.

Teresa was staring down at Winnie, but Winnie went on nonetheless. For some reason, she felt at ease talking to Janice, more at ease than she'd felt doing almost anything else for the last few weeks. "Well, this therapist I know always says that everything takes time. And she also says that anything worth doing is going to be hard and is going to hurt sometimes. And that you learn from your mistakes. Not that my mother— I mean, the therapist—is right all the time, but I guess she's not wrong all the time, either."

"I just know my mother's going to be so disappointed when she hears what happened," Janice said. "Or else she's just going to say, 'I told you so.'"

"She probably will say that," Winnie confirmed.

"Yeah." Janice let out a big breath. "She probably will."

"But you're the one who has to live your life. You can't go on forever blaming her or Brian for everything that's gone wrong, or waiting for them to tell you what you can and cannot do."

Janice kept talking and Winnie listened. She

took in every word, every silence, as if Janice were her oldest friend. Finally Janice sighed calmly and said, "Gee. Thanks. I feel better."

"You do?" Winnie countered in amazement.

"Well," Janice said, "I don't exactly feel like going dancing, but at least I think I'll make it through tonight." She laughed softly.

"Well, that's okay for a start, isn't it?"

"Yeah, I guess it is. Thanks."

"Thank you," Winnie breathed.

"Me? What are you thanking me for?"

"Never mind." Winnie slowly hung up, and as she did she thought about herself. She wondered if she and Janice weren't on the same road, waiting for other people to be the traffic lights in their lives. Then she looked up. David had joined Teresa and they were both staring down at her.

"I'm sorry," said Teresa with a funny expression on her face.

David looked equally perplexed, gazing down at Winnie and rubbing his chin.

"Sorry?" Winnie asked.

"I'm sorry we were so rude when you first came in," Teresa explained. "We just haven't got enough people working here yet. Anyway, you're so wet—and you looked so distressed—that I thought you'd come in for help. We didn't realize that you'd come in because you wanted to help out."

"To help?"

David nodded. "I hope that's why you came in. Aren't you a psych major from the university? We put up signs all over Blauman Hall asking majors to drop in this weekend and start to train as volunteers. A lot of people who were initially interested have given up. We sure could use someone like you. You can even get class credit for it."

"Of course, you still need a lot of training." Teresa smiled. "But we can tell that you have the instinct for it."

"You can volunteer for as many or as few hours as you want," added David. "Teresa's right. We really need help from more people just like you. You'd do a lot of good and, as you can tell, we're in desperate need of help."

It took a moment for Winnie to catch her breath. "I'll think about it," she finally said. "I guess I would like to help."

David grinned. "Thank you!"

"Great," said Teresa.

"Thank you." Winnie breathed a deep sigh of relief. She knew that *she* was the one who had just been helped.

Fifteen

·········•·········

At midnight the lobby of Coleridge Hall was quiet. For once no one was practicing scales or rehearsing in their tap shoes. There were no easels set up and no photographs drying over the back of the lobby couch. The lights had been dimmed and the creative-arts dorm looked like any other residence hall.

"It's a good thing there's no one here," Faith whispered as she led Alec through the lobby and toward the stairwell that led up to her room. Her borrowed velvet dress had dried stiff and her raincoat was still faintly damp.

Alec paused to look around, taking in the dorm lobby as if it were a room in a museum.

"I just mean that if the people in my dorm saw you here, there would probably be a riot."

Alec looked embarrassed, then followed her to the stairs.

Faith led the way up the concrete stairwell, feeling as if she'd just finished a fifty-mile hike. She stopped before she got to the second floor. She knew that Alec would be leaving first thing the next morning to go back to Los Angeles. If anyone happened to walk out into the hall and see him, it would only be a matter of minutes before the whole floor was up and out. For these last few moments, she wanted him to herself.

She leaned back against the railing and faced him.

Alec stopped climbing, too. He put his hands in the pockets of his raincoat and leaned back against the wall. "I'm sorry we didn't find your friend."

"I'm sorry, too. It was probably a long shot. Maybe Winnie's been in one place this whole time, with a new friend or some new guy. Or maybe she's not even in Springfield at all anymore."

"Maybe."

Faith's eyes met Alec's and for a moment they just looked at each other. She smiled sadly and realized that he no longer looked like a movie star to her. He just looked like Alec.

Alec hunched up his shoulders and shivered.

"I'm sorry you got so wet," Faith said. "This was a pretty strange way to spend your last night in Springfield. I hope you'll never meet another crazy student assistant who makes you drive all over town looking for her friend."

"You're not crazy, Faith. And you didn't make me go."

"I know." She laughed softly. "I just mean that I never expected you to help so much. I don't think Winnie will ever believe that Alec Brady drove his Mercedes around Springfield all night looking for her." A tear caught in her throat. "If I ever find her to tell her."

"You'll find her," Alec said.

"You think so?"

Alec just kept looking at her with those famous, soulful eyes. "I'm sure of it."

"How can you be sure?"

"Because anyone who has friends like you and KC would never leave them behind."

Unexpectedly, Faith began to weep. She put her face in her hands and then felt Alec take a step toward her. His arms slipped around her back and she rested her head on his damp shoulder until her tears eased.

"Oh, Alec," she finally managed to say, keeping her cheek against his shoulder. "Thank you."

"Don't thank me, Faith. I'm the one who should thank you."

"What for?"

Alec held her more tightly. "For allowing me to run all over town and not worry about who was going to see me."

Faith pulled back so that she could look into his face.

It took a moment before he would look back at her. "Thank you for letting me have an evening where I worried about someone else for a change, instead of just thinking of myself."

Faith wasn't sure what to say next. "I'm glad you came with us," she finally told him. "I just wish we'd found Winnie."

He reached up and brushed her hair away from her face. "You'll find her," he promised. "You'll find whatever you look for in life."

Alec leaned in and began to kiss her, and Faith suddenly felt as if she were falling or dreaming or swimming in light. A tiny part of her flashed on all the screen kisses she'd seen and how the couples came together so perfectly. But this kiss wasn't like that. Alec bumped her nose. She smiled and almost stepped on his foot. Then he laughed softly and they came together again. Finally it was perfect. It was a sweet, gentle kiss that Faith would remember as long as she lived.

Alec actually seemed self-conscious when he let her go. He took a step back down the stairs. "I guess I'd better head back." He cleared his throat. "I have to catch a plane first thing tomorrow morning."

"I know."

"I still have to pack and make some calls in the morning and turn in my car." He walked down a few more steps. "It's been a great night, Faith. I know you might not feel that way, but for me it really has been great."

"Really?"

Alec nodded. "Goodnight."

"Goodbye, Alec." Faith watched him as he continued to walk down. She tried to memorize his every step, so that when she next saw him on the screen, she'd remember who he really was.

When he finally got down to the lobby door, he looked back up at her and waved. "See you."

She smiled broadly, even though she doubted he would ever lay eyes on her again.

* * *

KC was struggling toward the lights of Coleridge Hall. The rain had finally stopped, but tears splashed down her face, nearly blinding her. Her poncho flapped and her long dress kept sticking to her legs. She had the most terrible feeling that Winnie was gone forever. Even as she raced through the Coleridge lobby, she remembered every slumber party and late-night talk she and Winnie had shared since junior high school. She missed Winnie so much that she barely knew how she'd go on with freshman year.

As KC hurried across the lobby, she knew that she would never forgive herself for snubbing Winnie and letting her down. She tried to think whether there was any place she might have forgotten to look. She'd gone back to the Beanery, Luigi's, and the Zero Bagel. She'd even checked the record store and the copy center that were open late.

"The hospital," KC gasped when she reached the door to the stairwell. Why hadn't she called there already? She thought of calling from the lobby phone, but she remembered that she had no money left. She had spent every cent taking a cab from Luigi's to the record store in the rain.

KC brushed away her tears and opened the

stairwell door, deciding that she would call the hospital from the hall phone by Faith's room. But as soon as she started up the stairs, she stopped. Faith was sitting on the top step in the stairwell, looking as dreamy and sad as if she'd just seen the ghosts of Heathcliff and Cathy walk past, arm in arm.

"What are you doing here?" KC flew up the steps and pulled Faith to her feet. "Come on, we have to call the hospital!"

"The hospital? Oh no! What happened?"

"Nothing. I mean something might have happened. I don't know," KC rambled. "But we haven't called there yet and maybe Winnie's hurt. Do you have any change?"

"In my room," Faith said.

KC pulled Faith up the last few stairs. KC's lips quivered and the tears started to fall again. Faith put her arm around her when they reached the top. They didn't speak, but held each other tightly as they pushed open the door to the second floor.

As soon as they stepped out on Faith's floor, they heard a soft voice singing a weird version of "I Heard It through the Grapevine."

"I heard it through the hotline . . . mmm,

mmm . . . Da da da da da da da da. Oh yeah . . ."

KC and Faith looked at each other, then began to run. They found Winnie, wet and disheveled, sitting with her back against Faith's door.

Winnie quickly looked away from KC, but gave Faith a sheepish grin. "Hi. I was lonely. Is it okay that I'm here?"

Faith and KC just stared at her.

"How was the party?" Winnie asked Faith. Then she picked at some dust on the floor and, not looking at KC, added, "How was the charity ball?"

"Winnie," Faith breathed.

"Winnie!" KC cried.

Faith and KC suddenly fell all over Winnie, hugging her and messing up her hair. They began to babble at the same time.

"Where have you been?"

"We've been looking everywhere for you!"

"Are you all right?"

"We've been so worried."

"Oh, Win," KC sobbed. "I thought I'd never see you again."

They finally drew back, and Winnie looked at them with amazement. "You noticed I was gone?" she asked in an innocent voice.

"Noticed you were gone?" KC and Faith repeated unbelievingly.

"We've searched the entire town for you," exclaimed Faith. "We thought you'd dropped out of school."

"We thought something terrible had happened to you. We were ready to call the hospital," said KC. "Alec Brady even came with us. He and Faith left the movie party because we were so upset."

Faith nodded. "KC skipped her charity ball because we were so worried about you."

Winnie's mouth fell open. "KC, you skipped that big charity thing with Courtney Conner because of me?"

"Of course I did," KC answered, starting to get angry. "What do you think I am? I'm not such a bored beauty that I was in the mood to go dancing with a bunch of stuffy rich people and eat pheasant, or whatever they served, when I found out you'd been missing for over twenty-four hours and no one knew where you were."

Winnie looked stunned. "And Alec Brady helped look for me? *The* Alec Brady?"

Faith nodded.

Winnie stared at them. Silent tears began to

run down her cheeks. "You mean you all decided that a wacko mattered after all?"

That was when they all began to weep. They hugged again and cried until the tears turned to laughter, then back to tears, then back to laughter once again.

"Hey, KC," Winnie stammered, "I think the water pump burst." She wiped away her tears, smearing them all over her face. Then she leaned closer to Faith and laughed. "Maybe I should cry over your raincoat. I think it could use another soaking."

They all laughed.

"I'd cry all over your dress, KC," Winnie went on, looking at KC's drenched black formal, "but it looks like it's already pretty wet. Hey, maybe that dress was meant to be worn in water."

KC laughed harder. The last time she'd worn the black dress had been at Winter Formal, when Winnie had pushed her into the swimming pool fully dressed. She wrung out a corner of the black fabric and fell giggling against Winnie and Faith.

Winnie held up her hands. "Let's promise not to cry anymore tonight! None of us can cry anymore. I don't want to cry for at least a month."

KC smiled and nodded. "And let's promise

never to let anything get in the way of our friendship." Tears began to slip down her cheeks again.

Winnie pointed at her. "You promised. No crying."

KC laughed. "I don't know if I can manage that right now. But the other promise, the one about us always being friends—that's the one that counts."

"Yes," Faith agreed in a very serious voice.

"Do you really promise?" Winnie asked one last time.

"I promise," said Faith.

"I *really* promise," said KC, as she hugged her friends.

Sixteen

"The exam will cover the Italian Renaissance in its entirety," Dr. Hermann lectured. "Multiple choice, plus short-answer and essay questions. You'll be responsible for all the information in the textbook as well as in the lectures, so be prepared."

The Western Civ students groaned, rose from their seats, and began collecting their things. Sticking her notes in her briefcase, KC waited for Winnie, Faith, and Lauren before walking out into the bright sunshine.

The four girls were in step as they headed past the library. The weekend rain had left a few puddles and a brisk breeze blew their hair in front of their faces.

"I can't believe I'm staying in school for a sadist like Dr. Hermann," Winnie chattered, popping a piece of bubble gum into her mouth. "He must give more tests than any other professor here. I bet he has a torture chamber in his basement at home." She jogged slowly, turning around to face the others and blowing big bubbles.

"He doesn't need a torture chamber in his basement," KC joked. "He's got one in his lecture hall."

Faith nodded. "Florentine domination, expansionism, oligarchies. Ugh. I'll never catch up on what I missed last week."

Lauren laughed. "I'd take the rack any day over another one of Dr. Hermann's exams. I'm really going to have to cram for this one. I didn't get any studying done while I was away. And I'll have to make up the hours I missed this weekend at my job."

Winnie cringed. "I don't think any of us got any studying done this weekend."

"Hey, Lauren, tell KC and Winnie how your weekend went," Faith insisted. "Tell them what happened with Dash and his folks."

"Yeah. What happened?" KC prodded.

"Tell us!" Winnie urged.

Lauren turned up the collar of her jacket as the wind picked up and they walked past the university bookstore. She stopped when they got to the end of the path and turned toward the journalism building. "There's nothing to tell," she said simply, her pale face looking radiant. "I was so nervous the first day that I barely said a word to anyone. But then Dash started arguing with his father about radical politics, and I couldn't stand not getting my two cents in. So pretty soon we were all arguing and having a great time."

Winnie applauded. "Let's hear it for not keeping your mouth shut!"

Lauren laughed and started walking away.

"Lauren, see you back at the dorm," Faith called.

"Let's meet when I get back from the newspaper office!" Lauren yelled back. "We can study and watch our old soap opera at the same time."

"Yes!" Winnie shouted.

"Okay," Faith agreed.

"See you later," Lauren called.

The three old friends walked on. They stopped on the student union patio, near the outdoor tables with umbrellas that fluttered in the wind.

KC hugged her briefcase and smiled at Winnie. "I guess I'm the only one who got a lot of work done this weekend. In spite of everything, my weekend was pretty productive."

Winnie blushed. "I'm glad my weird *Wuthering Heights* notes helped you. You could have called my version 'Heathcliff from the Underground.'"

"Well, my paper is very above-ground," KC said proudly. "I actually think it's pretty good."

"It is," Faith said. "I read it."

Winnie looked down at her boots. "Okay," she began. "Before we start this marathon study session for Hermann the Torturer, let's at least enjoy a major pig-out. I'd like to start with student union nachos and those chocolate frosted doughnuts."

Faith made a face.

"Sorry." Winnie shrugged. "I may be feeling a little better than I was last week, but old bad habits die hard." She thought for a moment. "Maybe that's what Josh sees in Sigrid. She probably eats nothing but carrots and steak."

Faith and Winnie started to go into the student union, but KC hung back. She checked her watch. "I can't stay to eat, Win. I have to go."

"Where?"

KC cleared her throat. "I have to go over to Sorority Row."

"What for?" asked Faith.

KC took a deep breath. "Courtney called this morning and asked me to come over and talk to her. I can just imagine what she's going to say."

Winnie put her hand to her forehead in a mock-tragic gesture. " 'You, KC, are banished from Tri Beta'," she pronounced, pretending to be Courtney. " 'Anyone who stands me up for the world-famous charity ball can never show her face on Greek Row again!' "

Faith giggled.

KC tried to laugh, but no sound came out.

"At least Courtney can't make you turn into a pumpkin at midnight," Winnie said, trying to be comforting. "And if you do, you can always hide out in my room."

"It'll be okay," KC decided sadly. "I did what I had to do."

"And as Winnie's mom says," Faith added, "now you have to take the consequences. Maybe it's for the best, KC."

"Maybe." KC lingered a moment, then started to go.

Winnie stopped her. "I'm sorry, KC," she said in a serious voice. "I know the Tri Betas meant a lot to you. I wish you could have become a sorority sister and stayed friends with me at the same time."

"I wish that, too." KC smiled bravely. "Don't worry about me. I'll see you both in a little while."

"Bye," Faith called.

"See you soon."

"Bye, Win," KC whispered as she walked around the student union and toward the gym. She passed the soccer fields and the football stadium, praying that her sacrifice would turn out to be worthwhile. Even though she loved Winnie, and would never turn against her old friend again, she wished that her lesson hadn't carried such a terribly high price.

"Oh well," KC sighed as she left the campus and strode toward Sorority Row. "Goodbye, future. Goodbye, business contacts and status and class." She turned onto the row, passing the Gamma house and Kappa Omega Phi. "Maybe I'll like taking over my parents' health-food restaurant. Maybe I'll even get used to sprouts and tofu and saying, 'Have a nice day.'"

But when KC stopped in front of the white Tri Beta house, and stared at the elegant three-story building with the widow's walk on top, she knew that she was losing more than a chance for a better business future. She was losing Courtney. Courtney wasn't just a status symbol or a contact anymore, KC had been starting to think of Courtney as a friend.

KC strolled up the front path, breathing in the sweet scent of daphne and freshly cut grass. She stared at the well-tended flowerbeds, knowing that she was probably looking at them for the last time. Then she said goodbye to the tall, beautiful house before knocking on the door.

Diane Woo, the Tri Beta vice president, opened up. She looked as refined and elegant as ever in a teal sweater and a midcalf-length paisley skirt.

"Hello, Diane. I'm here to see Courtney," KC managed.

Diane gave her a curious smile. "Come on in. Courtney's up in her room."

As KC followed Diane through the living room, she tried to keep her head high. Six or seven Tri Beta sisters were gathered, working on some group project that involved ribbon and tiny baskets. A few said hello or waved. All of them must have recognized KC from the disastrous tea party two weeks earlier. KC hurried across the room.

A moment later, Diane left KC on the second floor. KC swallowed hard as she raised her hand to knock on Courtney's door.

"Is that you, KC?" Courtney called from inside.

"Um, yes, it's me, Courtney."

"Please come in."

KC summoned her courage and entered. Courtney was sitting at her computer, wearing slacks and a red blouse. Her hair was held back with a tortoiseshell headband. She continued to type even after KC closed the door. When Courtney finally turned around, there was a cool, wary look in her eyes.

KC sat on Courtney's bed. Neither of them said a word. It took a moment for KC to realize that Courtney was waiting for her to explain.

"I guess you'd like to know what happened on Saturday night," KC began.

"I guess I would."

KC cleared her throat. "I know I owe you an apology. I'm sorry. I would never have backed out on a date like that, except that something truly urgent came up."

Courtney continued to stare at her.

"It involved my friend, Winnie," KC went on

nervously. "I doubt you remember her. You met her when we went to the audition—"

Courtney cut her off. "I remember Winnie."

"Oh. Good. Well." KC was getting more and more uncomfortable. Suddenly she just wanted to finish her explanation and run all the way back to the dorms. "Winnie was in trouble. She ran away because she was upset about some things that had been happening in her life. Just before I was supposed to meet you I found out that Winnie had been missing for a whole day and night. So Faith and I went to look for her."

Courtney's face began to change. Coolness was replaced by concern. "Did you find her?"

"Eventually. She's okay, as it turned out. But I thought something terrible had happened to her." KC put her hands to her face. "Oh, Courtney, I hated to miss that charity ball, but I couldn't go knowing that Winnie was in trouble. I just couldn't. I know you don't understand and that I was wrong to stand you up at the last minute, but I had to do everything I could to try and help my friend!"

Courtney still sat, staring at KC with her mysterious brown eyes.

Knowing that she'd said her piece, KC stood up and started for the door.

"KC," Courtney called after her.

KC stopped.

"Where are you going, KC?"

"Back to the dorms. It's okay, Courtney. I know I can never rush this sorority now. I'll just go back home."

"But one day soon *this* house might be your home, KC. Don't be in such a hurry to leave."

KC couldn't quite believe what she'd just heard. She slowly turned around. "What?"

Courtney cocked her head and sighed. "You seem to think that I'm going to cut you off because you helped your friend rather than going with me to some stupid charity ball." She began to smile. "What kind of a person do you think I am?"

KC didn't know what to say.

"I admire your loyalty, KC," Courtney stressed. "You know, loyalty is supposed to be a key element of our Greek system. Real loyalty, that is. That's why it's so important that we get rid of girls like Marielle Danner and encourage girls like you."

"Encourage me?" KC breathed. "Encourage me to do what?"

Courtney stood up. "To show interest in our house during spring rush."

"Me?" KC gasped. "You still want me to go through rush?"

Courtney laughed. "I'm afraid that's how the Greek system works, KC. You can't become a Tri Beta unless you go through rush. I can't promise you that rush will be perfect. But there's one thing I do know for sure."

"What's that?"

"I really want you to become a Tri Beta."

KC tried to contain her voice, but her grateful response burst out. "So do I!"

Seventeen

••

Two days later, Winnie stood on the sidewalk, staring up at the sign for the Crisis Hotline. The late-afternoon sun was high and bright. Winnie's miniskirt and over-sized man's sport coat were neat and dry. Her hair was still spiky, but no longer purple, since she had dyed it back to its original brown color. Everything was the same as it had been on that awful Saturday night, and yet it was all completely different.

"What is it that baseball dude said?" Winnie babbled to herself, trying to calm her nerves before walking in the hotline office. "It's déjà vu all over again."

When another girl, wearing a U of S sweatshirt, strode past Winnie and into the building, Winnie followed her in. Right away, Winnie saw Teresa Grey standing at the front of the room, where Winnie's mother had been standing such a short time before. Four other young people sat at the desks. Winnie sat in the back and waited for her first volunteer training session to begin.

"I want to thank you all for coming," Teresa announced, smiling at them all. "Since we're so short-handed, we'll be teaching you some shortcut techniques right away, so that those of you who are interested can answer phones this week, even if it's only to listen and give referrals."

Winnie nodded.

"Of course you won't be fully trained for some time," Teresa explained. "We can't tell you everything you'll need to know anyway. You'll need to learn from experience."

Winnie took notes. *Don't influence the caller. Listen. Assess. Ask open-ended questions. Relate personal experiences if relevant. Make nonjudgmental responses. Never try to handle a call that you know is beyond your abilities. Signal for help.*

"Any questions?" Teresa asked an hour later.

Winnie stayed through the questions and answers. She stuck it out at the hotline office all afternoon, reading articles supplied by Teresa and watching an instructional video. She made herself a crib sheet of referral numbers, reminders, and key phrases. After grabbing a slice of pizza at the gourmet pizza parlor down the street, she came back to help out and to study some more.

David was there when she returned from dinner. He remembered Winnie and shook her hand. "Great to see you again. I'm glad you decided to come back and take the training."

Winnie smiled. "Me, too."

Teresa was coaching another volunteer on his response to a fictional call, but she broke away from her lesson for a moment. "I thought Winnie could answer phones and even handle a few calls tonight," she told David.

"Good idea," David agreed. "If one more person hangs up on us because we put them on hold, I may just give up."

"No you won't," Winnie said. "I'll need you if I get a major crisis call."

David smiled and took off his jacket. "It's nice to be appreciated," he said, sitting down.

Winnie sat down at a desk, her notes laid out beside her. The first time the phone rang she automatically handed the call over to David, because she was too nervous. But then the lines got busier and Winnie became more confident. She gave information about the women's shelter to a woman whose husband had hit her. She listened to an elderly man who just needed someone to talk to. And she helped calm down a college student who'd found out that her boyfriend was seeing another girl.

Realizing that she was still tired from the ordeal of the previous weekend, Winnie started to pack up a little before nine. Then the phone rang, and she picked up the receiver one last time.

"Crisis Hotline," Winnie said. "Hello?"

No one responded.

Winnie figured the caller had decided to hang up. "Hello?"

Finally a male voice said, "Yes? Hello? You mean you really do answer your phones?"

Winnie couldn't hear him that well. There was the noise of traffic in the background, as if he were calling from a phone booth. He took his time before speaking again.

Winnie reminded herself not to fill in the empty spaces with her own words. She listened to the silence. She took a deep breath and waited for him to take the lead.

"Are you still there?" he asked.

"I'm here."

"Right. I, uh, feel kind of weird talking to someone I don't even know. I've never done anything like this before." His voice sounded tired and sad.

"That's okay."

"I don't know what I'm supposed to say."

Winnie sat up. "Just talk to me about whatever's bothering you. I'm here to listen."

"Okay." He coughed. "This feels weird, though."

"You don't have to—"

"No, no, that's okay. You see, I had this girlfriend."

"Uh-huh." Winnie put as much sympathy and interest into her voice as she could.

"And we broke up not too long ago." His voice cracked. There was another long pause. "I really miss her."

"I see."

"I've tried everything to cheer myself up. I've tried working. I even tried seeing another girl."

An eerie feeling started to creep up Winnie's spine. "Yes?"

"But nothing helps," he said. "All I do is miss her. My former girlfriend, I mean. She's kind of wild and different and wonderful, but . . ."

Winnie clutched the receiver more tightly and she curled over the desk. Her heart felt as if it had stopped. "But what?"

"But I love her," he stammered. "I'm in love with her, but I don't think it's going to work out. I feel like there's this huge hole inside me now and I don't know what to do."

Winnie cradled the phone. "Please, go on," she whispered.

"I don't think it'll do any good."

Just keep talking, she wanted to whisper. *It will do so much good for both of us if you just keep talking!*

Winnie had recognized the voice.

It belonged to Josh.

Here's a sneak preview of
Freshman Schemes, *the ninth*
book in the dramatic story of
FRESHMAN DORM.

Courtney Conner and the rest of the Tri Betas were cleaning for an open-house party. Suddenly the front door burst open and Marielle Danner stepped into the living room.

"Marielle, what are you doing here?" Courtney asked. "I didn't expect to see you in this house again."

"I have to speak to you about something, Courtney," Marielle answered. "It's quite important."

Some of the Tri Beta girls put down their brooms and dust rags. All of them continued to stare.

"We have a big night tonight, Marielle. I'll speak with you after we've finished cleaning up," Courtney said firmly.

"I don't think you want to wait that long, Courtney."

"What do you mean?"

Marielle walked into the center of the living room so that everyone could hear her. "I have information about a certain swim at a certain mountain lake," she said, putting her hands on her hips. "It's important information. If you don't want to hear it, I can tell everyone else on Greek Row instead."

Courtney felt as if she'd been punched in the stomach. She tried to maintain her dignity, but it took her utmost control. "Everyone, please keep working," she told her sisters. "We won't have much time to do anything once the lists are posted and Open House begins." She glanced at Diane. "I'll be back down in a few minutes," she assured her.

Courtney marched up the stairs, followed by Marielle. Once they were safely behind the door of Courtney's bedroom, Marielle sat down on Courtney's bed as though she owned it.

"I have something to show you," Marielle said,

digging in her alligator bag. "These just *happened* to come into my hands yesterday."

She handed a packet of photographs to Courtney, who began leafing through the stack. The awful feeling in Courtney's stomach grew worse. She began to feel faint. Each picture was worse then the next. All of them showed Courtney swimming at the lake with Phoenix, and it was obvious they were not wearing much. Courtney had the strange feeling that she was looking through scenes of a nightmare, one where she couldn't wake up.

She tried to keep her composure. "Where did you get these, Marielle?"

"I don't have to tell you."

Suddenly Courtney lost her patience. She began to tear the photos into tiny pieces, but Marielle acted as if it were a joke.

"I'm not a moron, Courtney," she insisted. "I have the negatives."

Slowly, Courtney absorbed the impact of what Marielle had said. It was called blackmail. She sank into her desk chair and stared blankly at Marielle.

"What do you want from me?"

Marielle crossed her legs and placed her hands in her lap, her smile broadening, "I used to want to get back into this sorority," she admitted, "but now that you've ruined the reputation of this house forever, I'm not sure I want to be part of it." Marielle sighed deeply. "On the other hand, I also don't want to see my poor ex-sisters become victims of your irresponsible behavior."

Courtney took a deep breath. "Marielle, what do you want!" she exploded.

Marielle remained unimpressed. She got up and flounced about the tiny room, picking up Courtney's stuffed animals and tinkling the charms on her bracelet. "It's bad enough that you can't be bothered to visit your own house's charity" was her next comment. "And you certainly don't have time for fraternity parties at the ODT house anymore. Everyone already knows how much you've slipped, but what's going to happen when these photos are all over Greek Row?"

"MARIELLE, WHAT DO YOU WANT!" Courtney yelled, her anger and fear mixing, until she began to tremble.

Marielle sighed again, relishing Courtney's agitation.

"I'll tell you what I want from you, Courtney," she answered, her twangy voice becoming serious. "You took something from me that I really valued—my membership in this house. Well, now that I've learned to be a little more assertive, I want you to understand what I'm going through. I want you to step down as Tri Beta president."

Courtney looked stunned.

"If you resign as president, I'll burn the negatives," Marielle continued. "Otherwise, you and this house will be the laughing stock of Greek Row."

Courtney swallowed, but didn't say anything.

"I'm going back to my lovely dorm room now," Marielle said in parting. "I'll wait one hour for your decision. If I haven't heard from you by then, and you haven't assured me that you will step down as president, I will pass those revealing photos to all of Greek Row."

Courtney felt so dizzy that she thought she might collapse. It took effort to steady herself.

Marielle sensed her near victory. "I can promise you one thing," she said, gloating, as she opened the door. "Once those photos are circulated up and down the street, no one will look at Courtney Conner the same way again."